IN THE SHADOW OF DIABLO
Mystery of the Great Stone House

A portion of the proceeds from this book will be
donated to the John Marsh Historic Trust for the
restoration and preservation of the John Marsh Stone
House, a part of the California State Park system.

Printed in the United States of America

First Printing, 2012

ISBN-13: 978-1475082920

ISBN-10: 1475082924

CreateSpace

www.createspace.com

Cover Design by Veronica Hanel

For Jackie, Ronnie, and Lise –
my family of muses

PREFACE

During the mid-eighteen hundreds, Dr. John Marsh was one of the most influential men in the establishment of California statehood. His life was filled with pioneering spirit, incredible heartbreak, and encounters with both sides of the law. His death was sheathed in mystery and intrigue.

Historical documents detailing his life and death provided the foundation for this story. The descriptions presented are an accurate, though general depiction of actual events. Naturally, many of the details required fabrication. It is my intent for the reader to gain insight into some extraordinary characters that were involved in a remarkable chapter of California history.

The legend around which this tale is woven is based on true accountings and recollections. Some readers may be able to discern fact from fiction throughout the book; others will use the End Notes to assist. All readers should be open to the possibility that this legend, like many around the world, is based on fact. So rather than the retelling of a past event, this story may be the prelude to a future discovery. Only time will tell...

Dan Hanel

ACKNOWLEDGMENTS

I wish to acknowledge the many individuals who so generously gave of their time. To Carol Jensen whose enthusiastic embrace of all things John Marsh helped overcome my initial inertia. To Kathy Leighton, historian extraordinaire, who allowed me liberal access to the East Contra Costa Historical Society's archives. To English teachers Mike Wood and Lisa Kingsford who graciously agreed to serve as editors – and who had their hands full. Finally to my wife, Jacqueline Hanel, whose helpful critique and wholehearted support encouraged me to fulfill my goal.

Thank you all!

CHAPTER 1

EXTRA COUNSELORS WILL BE on campus…
In nearly twenty years of experience with public education, it was the e-mail line that he most dreaded reading. It always meant one thing…tragedy.

His day began typically, as it had thousands of times before: waking-up alone, before dawn in his quiet suburban home; getting to the high school early, before most of the other staff; entering his classroom and firing up the computer.

This morning the computer took an agonizingly long time to come to life. He remembered the days not that long ago when he just let the thing go to sleep when leaving at day's end, but during this time of severe budget cuts in California, the school district's energy police were particularly vigilant about checking whether staff were turning off all unnecessary electrical items at night. He had already received one polite, yet pointed, e-mail reminding of this requirement, so he always turned everything off — computer, monitor, printer. It was annoying, but he knew it was the right thing to do even if the cost savings seemed miniscule.

The chime of Microsoft Windows coming to life called him back from a daydream. He clicked open his e-mail and began scanning through it as he always did first thing in the morning. He quickly deleted anything that resembled SPAM, wondering how it was that the incessant ads for erectile dysfunction always managed to get through the school's filters. He noted any communications from parents that needed a response and read messages from colleagues.

On this morning, however, it was easy to skip straight to one dispatch; not only was it from the schools' principal and addressed to the whole staff, but it was tagged with that familiar, though seldom used, bright red envelope signifying its importance.

"It is with a heavy heart," the message began, "… that I need to inform you that Brentwood High School lost one of our own last night. Alex Moreno was killed by a train just outside of town. It appears that it was a suicide. Many of your students knew Alex and may need to grieve. Extra counselors will be on campus and you can refer students for assistance. We will provide more details as we get them."

It was not the first time that he had experienced the death of a student. In fact any teacher that has been at it very long, especially in a large school like Brentwood High, with over two-thousand students, will have faced a student death; sometimes from cancer, sometimes from a car accident, and too often at the high school level, from a suicide. But this one hit particularly hard. So hard in fact, that the impact from reading the name literally set him back in his chair.

Alex was a student of his two years ago as a sophomore in biology. Later, as a junior and senior, Alex made a point of keeping in touch by dropping by his classroom to say 'hi' or occasionally eat lunch with friends. But it wasn't just that he knew Alex. He knew other students over the years that had passed, and while their loss was always heart-wrenching, it did not have the physical impact that this report had. It was not just Alex's death; it was his death by suicide. Suicide did not feel possible and the thought made him physically ill.

"Morning Mr. B." The friendly greeting from one of the 34 students that would soon enter the room for their first period class dragged him out of the trance and back into the moment.

THIS WAS HARRISON BARRETT'S fourteenth year as a high school science teacher. He had won numerous honors and awards for teaching excellence and was a shoo-in to be nominated for or to win Most Popular Teacher at whatever school he was working. He was the kind of teacher that kids felt comfortable visiting before school or at lunch time, not just because he was open to letting them hang out in his classroom, but because they felt he did not talk down to them.

Casual conversations with Mr. B were peppered with bad jokes and corny puns, but they were always at an adult level, which the teenagers appreciated. Harrison found out long ago that a sense of humor did wonders at building relationships with the students he was charged with educating; and if there were no relationship there would be no learning.

He also knew that his role was not to be their friend. Teens have plenty of friends. It was much more important to be a role model or mentor so the boundaries were always very clear, though they had been tested on more than one occasion, especially early in his career.

Harrison began teaching high school when he was twenty-two, just a few years older than some of the seniors. He was tall and nice looking, with a bright smile best described as a grin, dark hair and intense green eyes, and a slim, athletic build that was more in line with a tennis player than a football player. Certainly not a head-turning model, but what impressionable young teenage girl wouldn't be infatuated with the cool young teacher?

Older teachers and administrators at the time laid out a whole list of do's and don'ts for interacting with teen girls. Mostly it was don'ts. And the number one don't was *'don't ever be alone in a closed room with a female student!'* It didn't matter if nothing happened, all she has to do is *say* that something happened and your career could be over. This rule had been adhered to emphatically for these fourteen years. Mr. Barrett's open door policy was to have an *open door*.

These days Harrison worried much less about 'The Prime Directive' as he called it. He was well into his thirties and it didn't seem like the girls looked at him quite the same as they used to, though he was still a nice looking man and relatively fit for his age. He had a morning exercise routine that included martial arts, which he had been studying at one level or another for nearly twenty years.

During his late teens and twenties, he was a successful competitor in martial arts tournaments around the region, but as these events began feeling more about winning and less about the spirit of the art, he took to studying and training on his own, with occasional visits to various instructors that he thought could provide new insight. This routine kept him in good shape, even as the effects of middle age took their toll.

His hair was graying, earlier than he had hoped. Though he always thought it would be cool to be the science teacher with the long gray ponytail, genetics had other plans. So, with his once curly locks thinning and receding, he finally decided it was a losing battle and shaved most of it off. Fortunately this was a common style during this time so it was easy to play it off as being trendy, rather than just old.

He also gave up on wearing contacts in place of glasses. When he was younger, he was sure that women would prefer a man that did not look like the complete nerd that his science background already foretold. He considered laser surgery but it was out of reach on his teacher's salary. During his recent relationships, it did not seem to matter one way or the other, so he stopped worrying about it so much.

"Oh my God, Mr. B, did you hear about Alex Moreno?" Sasha squawked as she launched through the door into the classroom.

Harrison was not surprised that Sasha, another of his first period students, was already aware of the tragedy. She seemed to know everything that was going on about everyone. In fact it was she who told him about the 'little fling' that Mr. White in the math department was having with Mrs. Schneider in the PE department. Harrison, somewhat uncomfortable with the topic, deflected the conversation by asking to see her homework from the previous night, knowing full well that it was at least a ten-minute quest for Sasha to find anything in her backpack.

This time, however, Harrison was sure how she found out, but for the sake of appeasing her need to be the bearer of all gossip, he asked how she knew.

"Ally texted me on the way to school. Ryan Jorgenson texted her because his dad works for the police department and had to respond to the call last night."

"So I guess pretty soon the whole school will know," Harrison replied.

Sasha gave him the 'oh, duh' look that he was far too familiar with and added, "Well they will in the next couple minutes." She turned and walked toward her desk, head down and thumbs flailing at a speed that still amazed Harrison no matter how often saw kids texting.

"And remember to put that phone away when the bell rings or it gets confiscated." He was sure she heard him, even without the inkling of an affirmation in voice or body language.

The commotion as the rest of the class trudged into the room reminded Harrison that he still had a couple things to prepare for the day's lesson. The students settled into their seats and the start-of-school bell rang. Mr. B immediately took center stage. "Good morning everyone, I know most of you are aware, but for those who haven't heard, a Brentwood High student died last night".

He waited for the faint gasp from the few kids who did not get a text message, then continued, "Alex Moreno was a senior here and apparently committed suicide last night by stepping in front of a train. Some of you may know him or at least know of him, even though he was a couple years ahead of you. Please be mindful that this is going to be a very sad time on campus, especially for his friends and classmates. If you feel like you need to talk to someone, counselors will be available in the admin building. At this time, however, we need to carry on with class."

"So if we feel too emotional to work," came a comment from the front corner, "... does that mean we don't have to?"

By this time in his career, Harrison had become adept, a master really, at discerning the true intent behind a student's comments — who was the student, what was the context, how was it worded — it was much more of an art than a science that could be defined. In this case, he had no doubt that this comment was insincere and its only purpose was to draw a reaction from the class. Instead, it drew Mr. B's death glare.

The death glare was a tool that needed to be in every teacher's arsenal, but Harrison consciously whittled it to such a fine point that it pierced the shield of even the rowdiest and most non-compliant of students. He took particular pride in being able to silence multiple students with one death glare.

He wasn't sure exactly why he was so good at it. Perhaps the penetrating green eyes, or the slight squint coupled with clenched jaw. Maybe the head tilted down ever so slightly and the prolonged, motionless stare. He did know that the wait time holding the stare was particularly important. He can remember commenting to a rookie teacher he once observed that his *death glance* just did not have the required effect on changing behavior.

This time, the death glare resulted in the desired outcome, and the 15 year-old who made the inappropriate comment withered into oblivion. Harrison could tell that his students knew today's class would feel different. The bad jokes and silly puns would be missing and a somber, straightforward attitude would take their place. "You know the routine. Start on the warm-up question while I take roll."

CHAPTER II

THE COOL BREEZE FELT refreshing, even more so since he could not remember feeling anything cool for the past several weeks. Even the nights sleeping under the stars were warm and dry. It wasn't until he started following the banks of the large San Joaquin River that the air began taking on a different, more welcoming quality.

He dismounted and led his horse through thirty or forty feet of dense reeds until he found a small, rocky bank where it could reach water to drink without sinking in the mud. He pulled the crude map he had been using out of a leather saddlebag and squatted down on a large rock a few feet away.

These maps were popular seven years earlier when word spread that gold had been discovered not far from here. He remembered some of his neighbors back in Illinois talking about it. A friend even tried convincing him to join his journey west. "We'll be rich," he said. "I heard you can find gold nuggets the size of walnuts just lying in the hills, waitin' to be scooped up. Come on, Charlie, think what you'll be able to buy your ma when you get back."

Three things bothered him about that conversation so much that the thought of gold vanished from his mind for years. First, he was by nature a suspicious man. As a young boy his father taught him not to trust anything or anyone who seemed too good to be true. He still held firm to that attitude.

Second, he hated being called Charlie. His name was Charles, Charles Marsh, and anyone worth spending that much time with while seeking their fortune a half-continent away would know that. And third, the woman he lived with was *not* his 'ma'. Charles' mother died when he was seven years old, and even though he was very young and more than two decades had passed, he still felt the pain of missing her. The intensity had dwindled, but he knew it would always be with him.

His mother, Marguerite Deconteaux, was French-Canadian and Sioux. She was his father, John's, common law wife, since he could not legally marry an Indian. Charles' image of her had faded so much that he could only recall that she was very pretty with dark features and that she did not look like anyone else he met. Not like the Sioux his father spent so much time with, and definitely not like the other Europeans scattered about the small settlements within the Illinois wilderness.

Charles remembered, only faintly, receiving the news that his mother died. His memories were much more vivid about the months prior to her death. His father had gone back to Minnesota to lead the Sioux as they assisted the U.S Infantry and several state militias in preparation to battle Black Hawk, the Sauk indian chief who denounced a twenty-five year old treaty allowing white settlement of all lands east of the Mississippi. Black Hawk rallied factions of Sauk and Fox indians and began harassing settlers as he attempted to regain lands east of the river.

Charles and Marguerite were left to board, out of harm's way, with the Paintier family in Illinois who were friends of John's from his previous travels. It was here that they first met a young Abraham Lincoln, whom their father had befriended. John spoke highly of Mr. Lincoln to Charles, describing him as a man

9

of simple upbringing but of great intelligence and character. John Marsh himself was highly educated, having graduated from Harvard. He'd studied medicine, read profusely, and learned to speak several languages including Latin and Greek. And while John valued a man's intellect it was — as he preached to Charles — a man's character that made him most worthy of respect.

Charles took pride in relaying his father's feelings to Mr. Lincoln years later when they met shortly after Abraham Lincoln was selected as the United States Representative for Illinois.

Over and over Charles read the letters from his father detailing adventures in the wilderness. After his mother's death, these letters became the only contact with his father for months and even years at a time. He read them so frequently that he was sure he could still recite them from memory.

Dear Charles

I hope to soon join you and your mother. I fear, though, that it may be some time before I shall be released from my duties. The new Indian agent, a Mr. Street, has accused me of warning the Sioux leaders of his plan to meet with representatives of the Sauk and Fox tribes, who are their sworn enemies. It was with regret that I learned of the ambush and killing of these representatives by members of the Sioux.

All of Prairie Du Chien knew of this planned meeting, yet Mr. Street saw fit to place foremost blame on me. I have, thus far, convinced him otherwise, but I fear that I have now another enemy. There have been many killings in revenge by the Indians. I dare not

send for you to join me as the danger is too extreme. Mind your
dearest mother and tend diligently to your studies.

Your most loving father,
John Marsh

This letter was etched deeply into Charles' memory since it was the last letter he read together with his mother. He could tell, even at his young age, that his mother yearned deeply for her husband. She spent hours sitting in quiet solitude and on more than one occasion, Charles caught a glimpse of tears that were quickly wiped away when she noticed him watching. It was not until years later, when he was a teenager, than he learned she was pregnant during this somber time.

He could still feel the gentle kiss and warm touch of her hand on his face the day she left the Paintier home in Illinois and began walking, with one pack mule in tow, to join her husband back at Prairie Du Chien, Wisconsin.

Even clearer was the feeling of intense pain that seemed to pierce his chest as he watched her walk away. It was a pain that elevated to a searing burn when Mrs. Paintier read the letter from John Marsh announcing the death of his beloved wife and Charles' dearest mother. She had become so weak and exhausted from the journey that she went into labor and both mother and daughter died upon reaching the outpost.

CHARLES LEFT ILLINOIS and the Paintier's eleven years earlier to begin the trek out west. It had been even longer since he had any contact with his father. When Charles was just nine,

John Marsh was forced to flee the Northwest Territories after being charged with and found guilty of illegally selling guns to the Sioux, to whom he was so connected. John relayed to Charles that he was heading west along the Santa Fe Trail and would send for his son once established.

The final correspondence that found its way from John to Charles was after a period of many years with no contact. The letter was long and described adventures that were remarkable, even by the 'John Marsh' standards that Charles had grown accustomed to when his father fought during the Indian wars.

On the way to Santa Fe, John was captured by Comanche Indians, but then managed to escape. Subsequently, he found his way further west to the pueblo of Los Angeles in Alta California where he convinced the Mexican authorities that he was a doctor by showing them his Harvard degree. The fact that the actual degree designation was written in Latin and completely incomprehensible to the Mexicans meant that John could tell them it represented whatever he wanted.

John Marsh's facility for languages enabled him to become fluent in Spanish during his travels. This, along with his previous anatomy courses at Harvard and a brief apprenticeship with doctors back east provided more than enough credentials for him to be officially proclaimed a doctor, especially in this sparsely populated wilderness where a physician's services were desperately needed. And from that point forward, he became known as 'Dr. Marsh'.

Charles found the last bit of this story especially amusing, since he knew of his father's profound sense of integrity and thought about how he must have rationalized this small mistruth. It was not, however, this letter that lead Charles to head west. It was, simply, his overwhelming desire to reconnect with the only real family he had left. Perhaps this would finally give his life some purpose that had been missing.

He had heard of letters that his father had written to political figures back east telling of the great opportunity for settlement by Americans in the far west. Its seacoast provided many locations for developing trading ports and its rich, fertile soil was ripe for agriculture.

And it was his father's clear directions that guided the first wagon train back in 1841 along the California Trail toward the large ranch that he now owned further north. Years later, many more joined the venture west when gold was discovered.

The map Charles was using, however, was an incomplete reproduction purchased many years prior and included only a few of the most prominent landmarks as references. Upon descending the western slopes of the Sierra mountain range, he decided to pick what seemed to be the next most visible landmark, Monte del Diablo, and head for it. Perhaps someone, a prospector or trader, will have heard of his father and be able to give further guidance.

CHARLES STOWED THE WEATHERED MAP back in the saddle bag and lead his horse back through the thick reeds to firm footing. He wiped the sweat from his brow, mounted his horse and slowly angled toward the west and the rising outline of Monte del Diablo on the near horizon. This mountain was obviously not comparable in height to the Sierras, which he had traversed weeks before, but its prominence, jutting up several thousand feet from the surrounding flat landscape, made it visible from a great distance.

Within an hour, Charles' slow pace brought him outside a small Indian village. Huts made of reeds and grasses dotted the area and barely clothed or nude Indians glanced up as he strode by. Several women wove together some of the same reeds into baskets as younger girls watched them intensely.

Charles did not share his father's gift for languages, but he decided to try to communicate anyway. The sun was getting low and he was desperate to find proper shelter. Many months had been spent sleeping outside and Charles was fatigued from travel. A house, or any building, would provide a welcome respite.

"House," he stated loudly; louder by far than a typical speaking voice, which was common for Charles when trying to be understood in another language. To his dismay, one of the weaving women lifted her head and pointed to the slight southwest. Charles had no way of knowing whether she really understood what he was asking, but figured it couldn't hurt to explore. The worst consequence, he reasoned, would simply be another night sleeping under the stars.

As his horse sauntered around the edge of a stand of oak trees, he was so startled by the vision before him that he lurched backward in the saddle, causing his horse to buck and jerk, confused about the desires of its rider.

Charles regained control of the reins and rubbed his eyes clear, sure that he was delirious. But there it remained. As he moved closer, he muttered to himself and let a sly grin cross his face thinking of the Indian woman a short time ago. "This is not a house ... this is a *castle*."

Like Monte del Diablo rising from the landscape in the distance, stood a structure made entirely of stone. Every wall was composed of large rounded rocks piled one atop another and mortared together. Windows stacked three stories high and a large central tower soared sixty-five feet into the air.

A porch held up by numerous octagonal pillars and lined with white railing ringed the entire outside of the building just under the second floor windows. He had seen images of similar Gothic style buildings in books about Europe, but never could he have imagined that one would exist out here, in what could be described as nothing less than the edge of nowhere.

With curiosity in control of his mind as much as exhaustion was of his body, Charles dismounted and cautiously approached the entry. But before he could place a foot onto the steps, the door flew open.

Filling the entire doorway was the figure of a man, barrel-chested with gray hair, chiseled features, and finely dressed in a dark coat and white shirt. Charles could not help but notice the long rifle the man gripped comfortably in his right hand.

"State your business," boomed the man's voice.

Charles took a deep breath before replying so as not to let his voice waiver. "Looking for a place to stay the night. I've traveled from Illinois." Charles was hesitant to say more about himself or his purpose to a stranger with a gun.

"In that case, welcome," said the man, his voice softer than before, but still resonating with authority. "We'll have dinner and you'll be shown a bed."

"I'm grateful for your hospitality. My name is Charles."

"Dr. Marsh," responded the man.

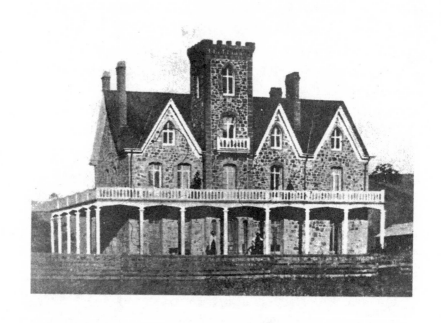

The John Marsh Stone House[1]

CHAPTER 3

THE CHATTER WAS NOTICEABLY less energetic as a dozen or so students sat in small groups around his classroom eating their lunch. Many teachers either fled their room or bolted the door, desperate for some down time before taking responsibility for another class of teenagers. Harrison, however, didn't mind. He enjoyed the opportunity to talk to kids in a less formal manner and knew the importance of finding out a little about their personal lives. Any morsel extracted from a conversation, perhaps a favorite hobby or insight into their family life, might serve well to better connect with and motivate a student later.

The kids in his room this day did not appear to be in a mood to speak with him, which suited Harrison just fine as news of Alex's death was still fresh on his mind. He was yanked out of his contemplation when the phone rang. "Barrett," he answered.

"How are you doing?" responded the voice on the other end. Harrison recognized it in an instant. The voice was feminine, but firm; and he always looked forward to hearing it.

Harrison first met Celeste Scott eight years ago when he was hired to work at Brentwood High. She taught Foreign Languages at the school for several years prior to that. Harrison was certain that everyone, himself included, remembered the first time they met Celeste. She was stunning.

Even now, in her mid-thirties, he knew there was not a teenage boy that was not crushed when they picked up their class schedule at the beginning of the school year and found out they were not going to have Miss Scott for a teacher. Harrison always

17

believed that if she were teaching Advanced Placement Calculus, the school's math scores would soar through the roof.

Foreign languages, however, were her passion. She taught Spanish, French, and German, and Harrison was sure she was well versed in several more. It was one of the reasons, he learned, that she decided to become a public school teacher; the long summer breaks allowed her to travel the world, which she did on a regular basis.

However, at the time of their first meeting, she was not Miss Scott; she was married. It had been almost two years since her divorce and he knew she was still recovering from the devastation. The proceedings were relatively public, as her ex-husband, who previously played professional baseball, apparently cheated on her. Harrison knew she was embarrassed and hurt. It was very painful for her to talk about, so he never learned many of the details.

Harrison wasn't married either, never had been. There had been a couple of long-term relationships, but he had not found the right connection with a woman to propose marriage. It was something that he missed deeply, but the dedication to his job usually kept him busy enough to prevent the occasional bouts of depression that overcame him, especially on weekends when the chaos of school was not there to distract from his loneliness.

While Harrison was as infatuated with Celeste as any other normal male, he knew she was way out of his league. He was, after all, just a pleasant, stable, high school science teacher. Nothing close to the handsome, wealthy men that she could, and did, attract. Though he was not sure exactly how it happened, they became good friends. They talked to each other frequently, usually just at work, but occasionally during a weekend outing to a movie or lunch. Time spent with Celeste, however, often stirred mixed emotions. While he loved her company - sharing the trials and tribulations of being a teacher - it always emphasized the incompleteness of his own life when, inevitably, he returned home alone.

"I'm doing OK, but I'm still in shock about Alex," Harrison continued over the phone.

"Can I talk to you after school?" Celeste asked.

"Sure, come on by about four. I'll have kicked out the last of the kids by then". Harrison thought about going to her room, but he knew she actually enjoyed being in his science classroom, with its lab tables instead of desks, interesting equipment scattered about, and live reptiles and amphibians housed in terrariums along the side counters.

HARRISON FINISHED HELPING two remaining students as they reviewed a few concepts together that would be covered on an upcoming test. It was about three-forty-five. He quickly organized some materials and wrote information on the front white-board for tomorrow's lesson. As he finished the last line with his back to the door, he heard her voice.

"Hi, Barre."

No one else called him 'Barre'. It was Harrison or Mr. Barrett or Mr. B. She started calling him this several years ago and he liked it. It felt more intimate than just using a first name. It was during one of their back and forth banters that he came up with the nickname he used for her. It had to be one syllable, like Barre, but her last name, Scott, was much too masculine to be descriptive of Celeste. The best he could do at the time was 'C'.

And it stuck. Fortunately, Celeste didn't seem to mind, though he wasn't certain whether she actually liked it or not.

Before he turned around, he took a deep breath, trying to hide the movement of his chest. While he had talked to her often over the past few days, he hadn't seen her. Their classrooms were not near each other and they belonged to different departments, so unless they made a conscious effort, they could go months without seeing each other. He knew that seeing her for the first time in a while would take his breath away, as it always did.

She walked toward the front of the classroom where he was laying down the dry erase pen and stepping out from behind his desk. As she approached, he caught himself soaking in the features with which he had become familiar.

Celeste was slim, but with the curves of a mature women. She had straight dark, almost black hair, and large, deep brown eyes. Her skin had an olive tone and Harrison assumed an Italian, or perhaps more exotic, ancestry, though he was not sure how her maiden name *Scott* was related. He had never gotten around to asking her about it, though he fully intended to one day.

She always dressed professionally, which he greatly appreciated. He'd been witness to far too many teachers who dressed causally, even sloppily. It worked for some of the really good teachers who could pull it off because they were older and already respected. When younger teachers did it, though, it appeared much more like they were trying too hard to be a kid's friend rather than their teacher. Harrison nearly always wore a tie.

As she approached, he also understood that if someone that looked like her dressed anything other than professionally, the rampant teenage-boy hormones would create havoc in her classroom.

Harrison could easily tell that Celeste was upset. Her usual sassy demeanor was much more subdued and he thought he could see the remains of a tear glistening in her eye. He walked directly toward her and held out his arms. She walked straight into his arms and they hugged. He had only embraced her a few times over the past couple of years, and those were quick hugs of congratulations for an award one or the other had won, or perhaps as the send-off for another school year coming to a close.

This hug was different. It lasted much longer and she held him much tighter. He responded in kind. This hug had emotion behind it and he took the opportunity to inhale her scent deeply. After a few moments they separated and she wiped away a tear below each eye, the way women do who don't want to smudge mascara, although Harrison did not think she was wearing any.

"Whew…thanks", she finally said, taking a deep breath to regain her composure.

"I take it you knew Alex pretty well," Harrison continued quietly.

"He's been in my French class for the past three years. He was also an officer in the Latinos Unidos club which I advise, so I saw him a lot."

Harrison pulled out a chair for her and they both sat at a student lab table. "But it's more than that, Barre."

"What do you mean?"

"When I read the e-mail saying he committed suicide I got sick to my stomach."

"You and me both," Harrison replied.

"Why?" Celeste continued. "I don't get it."

Harrison knew that she had read, as he had, numerous articles over the years discussing teen suicide. He knew it was easy to miss the signs of depression that could lead to it, especially if you just saw the person an hour or two a day. He also knew that having an intellectual discussion about it at this time was not going to be helpful. So he tried to console her as best he could. "You know there's no way to know exactly what's going on in a kid's mind."

Celeste paused, as if a myriad of thoughts were churning in her head. "The thing is, I did know him well …really well. He spent a lot of time in my classroom after school getting extra help and we talked often. He'd just been accepted to two or three of the colleges that he wanted to attend and couldn't stop talking about it. Being the first in his family to attend college meant everything to him."

"But you know," Harrison reasoned, "… there are so many other things going on in a teenager's life that can impact their emotions."

Almost before he could finish his thought, Celeste added, "He was well liked, had lots of friends and didn't seem too stressed out about school. The only issue I ever heard him struggle with was how to pay for college."

"How so?" Harrison questioned.

"His parents were hit hard by the lousy economy. Both lost their job and their house got foreclosed on. He was living in the third rental in two years. One of the things I was helping him with was filling out the applications for financial aid and even some scholarships that he qualified for. Kids that are looking forward to their future like that don't commit suicide."

Harrison waited for her to look up, then gazed directly in her eyes. "Sometimes they do."

"I need to know what he was thinking," Celeste firmly stated.

"What do you mean?" Harrison replied.

"I've got to figure out why he did it. There's no way I'm going to sleep at night without getting some sense of why he felt this was the only way out. And you're going to help, right?"

As his mind worked on processing what she just asked and what it would mean for him, his mouth could only utter, "uhhhhh."

"Great," Celeste confirmed. "I'll talk to some of his friends and other teachers to see if they noticed anything, and you do the same. At some point, well after the services, we'll want to talk to his parents."

Harrison was distraught over Alex's death and very much wanted to know why he killed himself, but without finding an actual suicide note, which he presumed they wouldn't, it would be next to impossible to decipher what was going on in this young man's brain that filled him with so much despair. But it also meant, he rationalized, that he would be spending more time with C, and if his friendship could help comfort her in some manner, then he would do whatever he could.

CHAPTER IV

September 3, 1856

THE MAN HAD ALREADY turned back into the house by the time Charles reached the steps to the doorway. "Doctor *John* Marsh?" he questioned anxiously.

"That's right," the man replied without looking back.

"Father...it's Charles."

The man instantly froze. As he slowly spun around, Charles could see that he still wore the grimace that appeared to be permanently etched onto his face. He thrust the butt of the rifle onto the floor and bellowed, "my son's dead; been dead for years."

"Well that's unfortunate," Charles retorted. "If I had known I was dead, I wouldn't have spent all this time looking for you."

John Marsh walked directly to the stranger and stopped within inches of his face. Charles was not sure whether he was about to be hugged or hit, so he stood motionless. John looked closely into Charles' eyes, squinting just a bit, as if trying to bring into focus the young man that he had last seen so many years ago.

Charles searched his brain for something he could say that would instantly convince his father who he was, and in the moment the best he could come up with was ... "Mr. Lincoln sends his regards. I spoke to him just before heading out west and told him how fond you were of him back when the two of you roomed together."

"Take off your boot." John demanded.

Charles stared dumbfounded at the request. "I beg your pardon…"

"Take off your boot and sock."

Charles, still utterly confused, did as directed. "I don't understand why …"

"My son has unusual toes. Now show me your foot or get the hell out of my house!"

Charles staggered to keep his balance while lifting his left foot. Still taken aback by the request, Charles was anxious until he realized the reason. He never thought about his webbed toes, but clearly, his father remembered. John bent down slightly and cocked his head, squinting again to bring Charles' foot into focus.

Charles felt his father's hand clasp the back of his head and witnessed the shimmer of tears form in his father's eyes; tears that he was sure were very, very rare, and perhaps had not been shed since his mother died. John pulled Charles' head close to him. "I was told you were dead. The letter said you were dead. I wrote for you to join me and they told me you were dead."

Although Charles knew that he looked very different from the last time his father had seen him, he now understood why it was so hard for his father to accept. "Well, as you can see, Father," Charles whispered, "I'm very much alive."

John pulled Charles in close with the hand that was still behind his head and swung his other arm around his back in a full embrace. Charles quickly flung both of his arms around his father and the two men held each other. They did not speak and they did not cry, though both were forced to wipe the moisture from their eyes when they finally separated. Charles noticed that the permanent frown on his father's face had lifted ever so slightly.

THE REUNION WAS INTERUPTED by a woman entering the room. She was short and plump and looked similar to the Indians from the village nearby that had directed Charles to his father's house, however, she was wearing a simple dress that appeared Spanish in style. She said something to John in a language that Charles did not recognize. John responded in the same language and she left the room. "Supper is ready. Let us eat and become....reacquainted."

John called out to two men that were in a back room of the house. This time Charles recognized the language as Spanish. Charles could understand his father giving directions to one of the men who was named Felipe, though he could not make out everything that was said. "My vaqueros will tend to your horse."

Father and son sat down to dinner together for the first time in decades. Charles told of his journey west. He headed toward the Rockies, as his father had done along the Santa Fe Trail, stopping to work for periods of time in various small towns in order to replenish supplies. Eventually word came of gold in California. The settlers he met in Kansas and Colorado talked of the California Trail, a quicker path over the Sierras that someone named John Marsh wrote about.

Charles started out for California as quickly as he could gather enough money and supplies. The path over the Sierras was difficult, but the summer weather was good and the journey smooth. Charles told of hearing fragments about his father's exploits, which mostly involved trying to influence politicians and the like. The talk was of the importance of settling the far west and eventually including California into the United States. John listened intently, still stunned by his son's rebirth, but also grateful that he was there and that he had grown into a fine young man.

Then it was John's turn to give accounts of his time in California. He left Los Angeles in 1837 and headed north to Yerba Buena to find land to purchase. Approximately sixty miles east of San Francisco, he found the property he had been looking for and quickly purchased the 17,000 acre Rancho Los Meganos from Jose Noriega who was granted it from the Mexican government.

The Rancho extended from the base of Monte del Diablo to the banks of the San Joaquin River and included fertile soils for growing crops, wide expanses of grasslands for raising cattle, miles of wetlands along the riverbanks, and large areas covered with sand dunes, for which the Rancho was named.

As he did with the Sioux back in Prairie du Chien, John took a great interest in the Indians. Most natives who lived in the villages on or near his property were Miwok, speaking a dialect of the Costonoan language that other tribes in the area used, including the Bulbones and Ohlone. John's tremendous skill with languages enabled him to quickly learn to communicate with the Miwok.

His medical knowledge was invaluable and much of his time was spent treating sick or injured Indians. In turn, they worked the fields and built an adobe house where John lived until just three weeks ago, even though the Great Stone House was finished many months prior.

John paused and Charles could tell he was reflecting about something unpleasant. "Why didn't you move in right away?" continued Charles, confused that his father would go to all the trouble and expense to build such a magnificent structure and then not inhabit it immediately.

Without looking up, John quietly replied, "later."

THE TWO MEN LEFT the dinner table where Charles had just finished the finest meal he could remember in years, stuffing himself with a huge beef steak and fresh vegetables. They eased into two large upholstered chairs in an adjacent room. John again looked distant, as if searching his mind for which memories he should share now and which he should hold back.

"I pay the Mexican cowboys, the vaqueros, to work the cattle. Best damn horsemen I've ever seen. It's the Mexican government that I could do without. Fifteen, maybe sixteen years ago, Governor Alvarado threw me and every other United States citizen he could get his hands on into jail."

Charles was shocked at the revelation that his father had been imprisoned. "For how long?" Charles inquired intently.

"About a month," John replied. "I had written some letters back east telling of the opportunities out here. Alvarado thought we were planning some kind of rebellion against Mexico. I believe he heard that I sent word of a passage over the Sierras straight to California and he must have been worried. Turns out he was right to be worried; I just didn't know it at the time." Charles knew that his father was referring to the Mexican-American war that began some years afterward and didn't end until 1848.

28

"Once I realized that California joining the union was inevitable, I tried everything I could do to assist in a peaceful transition," John insisted. "Others, however, were not so inclined."

Felipe, the vaquero from earlier in the evening, entered the room and explained something in Spanish. Charles could tell it was important and the vaquero looked agitated. John also took on an unsettled demeanor as he and the vaquero had a brief conversation. As the vaquero left the house with purpose, John turned to Charles. "Damned squatters. Ten miles to the east, twenty men setting up camp."

John rose from of his chair and began a slow pace around the room. "At first the squatters were just an occasional nuisance. Now, they have become a great thorn in my side. They trample fields without a care and kill cattle for food. Some years ago we had to fight off an attack on my very home." Charles could tell his father was extremely upset and assumed he sent his vaqueros to deal with the squatters. He wondered to himself *how* they would be dealt with, but chose not to question.

Charles lifted himself out of his chair and walked to a window. Night had fallen. In the darkness, small campfires were visible sprinkling the landscape both near and far from the stone house. "Tell me more, Father. What happened after the war?"

John walked to an adjacent window and looked out as if to peer back into the past. "That's when it really got interesting, my son. Only days after the treaty was signed with Mexico and we became Americans gold was discovered not far from here."

Charles glanced over at his father and with a somewhat sly, knowing smile said, "So I heard."

John returned Charles' glance and replied, "Oh, I did my share of looking." He turned back to gaze out the window and after a short pause said, "... with some success."

Charles could not help but behold impressive structure in which he was standing. *Was this built with gold,* he thought to himself. *Could his father possibly have had more than 'some' success?*

John added, "...and then they came. And they kept on coming. I could not have predicted the impact gold would have on settling California. For so many years, I preached about the wealth and fine living to be had from this land through crops and cattle. Yet that gold did more to persuade easterners than the combined efforts of every letter or article I ever wrote. And, of course, they had to eat. My cattle are feeding miners throughout California and my orchards provide them fresh fruits and vegetables. Now that you're here, Charles..."

That was the first time since Charles arrived that his father called him by his name, and it felt good.

"You will need to learn the business of operating a ranch. Having your assistance after all these years will lift a great burden. I have much to tell you."

The warmth that Charles felt moments ago when his father used his name was now a roaring blaze. When Charles began his journey in search of his father, his only goal was to find him and reconnect even if just for a moment. But now, to receive so much more was overwhelming. Charles was exhausted, yet the thought of sleep was far from his mind. He felt both thankful and disappointed when his father remarked that it was time to retire.

John said something loud in the Indian language. The plump women entered the room and led Charles upstairs to a bedroom. He was almost giddy with the sense of sleeping in a soft bed. As his head finally rested on a pillow, he was filled with contentment. He had not just found his father... he had found his life.

John Marsh and Miwok on Rancho Los Meganos[2]

CHAPTER 5

A WEEK HAD PASSED SINCE Celeste asked Harrison to help figure out why Alex committed suicide. Harrison was not exactly sure how to go about getting answers but he knew it was important to her and had promised to help.

He listened in on conversations that students who knew Alex were having, hoping to pick up some fact that might shed some light. He talked to a few of Alex's other teachers to get a feeling for whether they noticed anything about his behavior. He met with Alex's counselor who looked at recent progress report grades and described some of the activities Alex was involved with during his senior year. Nothing seemed out of the ordinary. No indications of someone who was depressed or overly stressed.

Harrison agreed to meet Celeste at Starbuck's Saturday morning to share what, if anything they found. When he arrived, she already was there, sipping her usual caramel macchiato. He ordered a mocha and sat down with her at a small corner table.

"Nice to see you," she smiled.

"And you," he replied. "How are you doing?"

"I'm OK, just frustrated. I've talked to everyone at school I can think of and no one had any inkling that Alex was considering something like that," Celeste continued. "How about you, any ideas?"

"Nope, I'm as baffled as you are. His counselor said he was on track with college applications. His most recent progress report grades were good; no evidence of any kind of bullying or harassment", Harrison responded. "She also said he was really enjoying his community service project. Apparently, Alex let her know that even though he was not looking forward to the forced volunteerism that was required of all seniors, he became very interested in the project he was involved with and couldn't wait to go back each week."

"Doesn't sound like someone who was contemplating taking his own life," Celeste pondered as she took another sip. "What was his community service project?"

"Something he was doing with the Brentwood Historical Museum. Not sure exactly, but based on what he told his counselor, he was really getting into it," Harrison answered.

"Well," Celeste said inquisitively and with a slight raise of a brow, "… you got time for a visit to the museum?" knowing full well what Harrison's response would be.

"I suppose," he finally replied. "But I'm driving."

THE MUSEUM WAS LOCATED on the far eastern edge of town, but it took only twenty minutes to get there. In the last twenty years, Brentwood had grown from a rural farm town with just one stoplight into a thriving suburb, complete with shopping mall, multiplex movie theater, and *many* stoplights. Yet, even with its rapid increase in population, the city still managed to keep a small town ambience, and it still did not take long to get from one end of the city to the other.

As they approached the Brentwood Historical Museum, Harrison noted the entrance plaque that described the building. It was a refurbished farm house from the early nineteen hundreds; wood siding and a front porch, all painted white. He admired the hardwood flooring and paneling inside the house and suspected they might be original.

The two teachers approached an elderly woman who was seated behind a table reading a book. Harrison thought to himself that historic museums always seemed to be run by elderly women and wondered if there were any that weren't. He reasoned she was probably a volunteer since these places never had much of an operating budget. It's probably why they agreed to use high school students that needed to complete community service hours.

"Excuse me, Margaret?" Celeste began, as she read the woman's name from her docent badge. "I was wondering if you could help us for a moment."

"Well, of course," Margaret smiled. It was apparent to Harrison that this museum was not going to be on any tourist maps of the area and he wouldn't be surprised if he and Celeste would be the only visitors the entire day. He figured most of the people that came here were elementary school classes on field trips. Margaret seemed pleasantly surprised to have guests. "What can I do for you?" she continued.

"We were wondering if you knew Alex Moreno, the high school student that was doing volunteer work here?" asked Celeste.

"Oh, my gosh, yes," Margaret responded. "When I read in the paper about his death, I was heart-broken. He was such a nice young man. Very polite and worked very hard."

"I'm Harrison and this is Celeste. We were his teachers." said Harrison as first Celeste, then he, shook her frail hand carefully. "It was very tragic and we've all had a difficult time trying to understand what happened."

"Which is why we're here," Celeste continued. "We were hoping to learn something about what he was doing before his death. Do you happen to know what type of work he was involved with here?"

"Oh, yes, yes. I coordinated the work for him. He was very helpful. I can show you." She led the two into a restored early 20th century library. Margaret pointed at a desk to one side of the room covered with old books, papers, and photos. On the floor were three large cardboard boxes that looked as though they had been in storage longer than Harrison had been alive.

"Alex was organizing a collection of historical documents and photos. Probably kind of boring for most teenagers, but after about the first month, he told me he really enjoyed it. The Historical Museum was thrilled to have someone take the time to catalog these pieces that have been in hiding for many years."

"May we take a look?" Harrison asked.

"Of course," Margaret responded. "However, you'll need to wear gloves. Many of these artifacts are from the eighteen hundreds. Alex was working with a collection donated only a few months ago from the estate of Alice and William Camron."

"What types of items are in the collection?" Harrison inquired.

"Oh my goodness," Margaret said enthusiastically, "…wonderful things belonging to John Marsh, her father. He was one of the first white settlers in California, definitely *the* first in Contra Costa County. All the land that Brentwood and many of the surrounding cities are built on used to be part of his ranch. He had a lot to do with getting California statehood back in eighteen-fifty."

Celeste took the seat behind the desk and put on a pair of the white gloves that Margaret brought them. "I've heard the name, but I must admit I don't know much about him." Celeste turned her focus back to Margaret. "Would it be OK if we take a little while to look through these things"?

"Certainly, take your time. Alex was very interested in this album." Margaret placed her hand on a large, leather bound book held closed by two ornate brass clasps. It looked like a cross between a photo album and a journal, but one that had been around for a hundred or more years. "I'll be at the table in the entry if you need anything," Margaret said as she turned and shuffled out of the room.

"OK, where to begin?" Harrison queried.

"How about you start with that album and I'll start with one of the boxes," Celeste replied. Harrison squeezed on a pair of the white gloves, which seemed to be sized for a woman rather than a man, and began thumbing through the album.

THEY CHATTED AS THEY SEARCHED, small talk, mostly about school and how classes were going. About an hour passed before they took a break to brief each other on what they found.

"Well, anything interesting in your boxes, C?"

"Lots of interesting stuff. Just the fact that this is all from the mid-eighteen hundreds makes it fascinating. Some photos of John Marsh relatives, some letters where he writes to people about California, some documents that look like receipts for goods received - apparently he bought an ox yoke and two ox bows all for twenty-four dollars in eighteen fifty-two. I don't even know what an ox bow is," Celeste exclaimed.

"It helps make the ox's hair look pretty," Harrison responded without missing a beat.

Celeste glared at him the way she always did when he made one of his bad puns.

"Alright then, Mr. Barrett," Celeste said sarcastically, still reeling from the comment, "how about you; anything important?"

"Yes, as a matter of fact," Harrison replied with a faux air of superiority. "The only problem is I can't read half of it." Celeste looked at him quizzically. "This book that Alex was so interested in is more like a journal. It's got writings from John Marsh, as well as drawings and diagrams, some photos. The unusual thing is that parts of it are in other languages."

Harrison laid the book in front of Celeste and leaned close. "These pages, here, appear to be written in Latin. There are a couple terms here and there I can pick up from their root word, but most of it I have no idea about. These pages look like Spanish, which I also don't speak...or read. And then these pages ...," Harrison flipped to several particularly well-worn pages. "They are in some language I've never even seen before."

As a foreign language teacher, this especially intrigued Celeste. She read through the Spanish sections and translated for Harrison. Most were notes or perhaps drafts of letters to officials referring to John Marsh's property or purchases. She could decipher a bit more of the Latin than Harrison, but not enough to make sense of. The unknown language also baffled her. She was familiar with many languages around the world even if she wasn't fluent in them, but this was like nothing she had ever seen.

"My guess," she continued after a long delay - Harrison visualized the gears churning in her brain as she worked through the possibilities - "is some kind of Native American. You figure this guy was living out here at a time when there were still lots of

Indians in the area. Likely he learned to speak and write it."
Harrison figured this sounded as plausible as anything else.

They searched through the documents for another hour or so finding many similar types of artifacts. The one item that remained unique was the book with the languages. Everything else seemed like ordinary artifacts that would be typical in a history museum.

But even the book didn't seem that important to them. It was unlikely that Alex could read most of it. Celeste was aware of his foreign language skills and he had to work hard to get a decent grade in the French class she taught. He was already fluent in Spanish because his parents both spoke it, but probably couldn't read it very well since many children of Mexican immigrants don't practice reading and writing in their native language. They could not imagine why he would be so interested in that particular book.

THE TEACHERS LEFT THE MUSEUM with no better understanding about what drove Alex to suicide. The walk back to Harrison's car in the parking lot was silent. Harrison followed Celeste to the passenger side door. Celeste looked back at him, confused. He then reached around her and opened the car door.

During five years of marriage, Celeste could not remember one time when her ex-husband ever opened a car door, or any door, for her. She appreciated the gesture and shot him a quiet smile.

"Well?" asked Harrison

"No clue," Celeste replied.

"Yeah, me neither."

CHAPTER VI

September 4, 1856

THE MORNING SUN BREACHED the bedroom window and Charles awakened from his long, comfortable sleep. He was not only feeling well physically, but emotionally was as content as he had been in years. Roosters crowed in the distance and the welcoming aroma of breakfast wafted up from somewhere downstairs. His thoughts instantly returned to the happy, though short-lived, days when he was a young boy in Illinois; waking in the morning to the smell of his mother's cooking, then joining his father at the table to partake.

Charles had to make a conscious effort to pull himself back to the present. He knew his mother was gone forever, but his father was here now. Something about that made him feel complete, as if a missing limb miraculously reattached, allowing him to be fully functional for the first time since being a young boy.

Charles dressed and followed his nose downstairs to the kitchen where the plump Indian woman was preparing eggs and pork. She motioned him to the table in the next room where his father already sat.

"How did you sleep, Charles?" John questioned, looking up briefly from some papers in which he was engaged.

Feeling emboldened this new morning, Charles responded, "damn good." John did not react.

Something again was said in the language Charles did not understand and food was brought to the table. Charles indulged in another full meal and the two men chatted, mostly about the past, retelling stories that were shared in letters many years ago. The conversation soon dwindled and they ate the rest of the meal in silence. Charles quietly observed the man across from him; a man that was his father, but also, Charles realized, a complete stranger.

They finished the meal and John advised Charles to get himself ready to view some of the ranch property by horseback.

CHARLES WAS ANXIOUS and met his father at the stable a short time later. As they began the tour, Charles was immediately startled to observe just how many Indians were living, not just on the property, but very near the Great Stone House.

John led Charles through a small village, a different one from where he got directions the day before, but of similar style. Numerous small huts were scattered, made of tules or reeds taken from near the river, and there were a few larger structures made of the same material. Chickens and goats roamed the area and as their horses walked slowly through the village, Charles focused attentively on many of the women smashing something with a rock.

Apparently noticing Charles' curiosity, John piped up, "I call them the Pulpones. They are a very peaceful and helpful people. Those women," John nodded toward the ones smashing with the stones, "...are crushing acorns. They make a paste that they eat with everything. Worst god awful stuff I've ever tasted," John added with a grimace.

John stopped several times to converse with some of the men in their language. Charles could not help but feel that it was an almost fatherly tone in which he spoke, very different than when he talked with the vaqueros. He seemed to be genuinely concerned about the welfare of the natives.

Near the end of the village, John dismounted and ducked into a hut. Charles was unsure of whether to follow, but curiosity overcame him. Inside was a woman with a young child wrapped in a blanket. The floor was dirt, but much was covered with mats made of the reed material.

John attended to the small child who appeared ill, suffering a cough and runny nose. He said some things to the Indian, obviously the child's mother, and she responded. John left the hut and took a small bottle out of his horse's saddlebag, poured a small amount of liquid into a spoon and fed it to the child. Something else was said to the mother and then both men left. "I care for them and they care for the fields," he said matter-of-factly as he remounted his horse.

They rode at a leisurely pace for several more hours. Through orchards of plums, peaches, and apples. Through fields of wheat and corn. Through ranges of cows, pigs, sheep, and chickens. Charles watched vaqueros working to rope and brand a calf and others caring for horses.

"About 40,000 acres now," John boasted.

Charles nearly choked. He could barely conceive of that amount of land, much less grasp that it all belonged to his father.

"In truth, Charles, it would be a paradise if not for the damn thieves and rustlers," John said. "I lost twenty more head last month. We caught four men; tried 'em and hung 'em."

Charles had a momentary notion to question his father about the 'trial' that the men received; was it fair, was there a judge, were the men represented; but he knew that justice in the far western frontier was not always what he was used to back east, so he let it drop.

It was early afternoon when John stopped and took a quick look at his pocket watch. "We'll have to see the rest another day. Time to head back to the house, they'll be here soon."

Again Charles found himself pondering his father's words. This time there were two things that rattled around in his head, 'the *rest* of the property'? How much more could there be? They had covered quite a distance already so Charles was intrigued to find out what else was contained within the boundaries of Rancho Los Meganos. But the second thing his father said made Charles even more curious, '*who* will be here soon'?

Charles thought seriously about questioning his father regarding the arrival of this person whom, apparently, he was anxious to see. Rather, Charles decided to let it unfold. John picked up the pace of his horse to a quick trot and Charles followed.

BACK AT THE STONE HOUSE, the two men sat relaxing on the second story porch. Charles questioned John non-stop about the tour of the ranch. How many head of cattle? How much were pigs sold for? How were they transported? What was the best way to prevent rustling? And John seemed only too happy to answer – but whether as a father or as a business partner was unclear to Charles.

In the middle of one of Charles' questions about growing grapes, John suddenly stood up and stared out to the west. "They're here." he said enthusiastically,

John quickly headed back inside the house and made his way down stairs and out the front door leaving Charles with the sense that his father suddenly forgot he was there. Charles followed behind, his curiosity piqued about who this could be.

Rounding a ridge was a small black buggy pulled by a single horse. As it neared the house, Charles could make out the figure of a woman at the reins. A moment later, he saw that she was somewhat older, perhaps even older than his father. A vaquero helped the woman down from the buggy and John stated, "That is Mrs. Thomson, a dear friend of the family."

But as Charles walked over to make her acquaintance, a young girl who looked to be no more than four years old, bolted from the back of the buggy, not waiting for the vaquero to assist. She leapt to the ground racing straight toward John who simultaneously skipped down the steps from the house toward the girl - and the two embraced.

Charles stood dumbfounded about whether to continue toward the women or toward his father and the little girl. John interrupted his dilemma by announcing, "…and this," putting his weather worn hand on the back of her blonde, nearly white hair "… is your sister, Alice."

The words were as foreign to Charles as the language of the Pulpones. He heard, *Alice*, "OK," Charles reasoned to himself, "Alice must be that little girl's name. But what was that other word he said right before… *sister?*" Charles searched his mind for a definition of this word. Surely, it must be Indian, or perhaps Latin, and he couldn't possibly know what it meant.

But he did know. His father had a daughter. A young daughter. But that meant ... he had wife. Another wife, that is; someone other than his mother. Where was she? This woman he referred to as Mrs. Thomson couldn't be this little girl's mother. The questions raced through Charles' mind as he considered all possibilities.

John walked Alice to where Charles still stood motionless. "Alice, say hello to your brother, Charles," John said softly to her.

"Hello," Alice obeyed decisively.

"A pleasure to meet you, Alice," replied Charles as he reached out his hand. Alice grasped his hand and gave him a firm handshake that thoroughly startled Charles by its confidence. Her eyes were the most intense deep blue color he had ever seen and her grin was so infectious that he couldn't help but smile. Her other hand was wrapped around John's leg and Charles could tell that she was completely attached to ... her father. And he appeared to be completely entranced by her.

IN THE HOUSE THE TWO men sat, each with a glass of wine poured to celebrate Alice's arrival home. "She's grown a lot in the month she's been away with Mrs. Thomson," John began, realizing that Charles must be aching to get more details. He appreciated Charles' patience in not pursuing questions right away. This was an important quality in a man, and John was glad it was a trait possessed by his son.

"Her name was Abigail Smith Tuck," John continued after a lengthy pause as he watched Mrs. Thomson tending to

45

Alice and helping her organize clothing unpacked from the trip. "After your mother died, it was of no importance to me to have another wife. My work was my companion. When I first made acquaintance with Abby, she was a girl's school principal in San Jose and the smartest woman I'd ever met. Gentle and pretty. We married after just two weeks. Alice was born a year later....but it was I who felt reborn. When I learned that you had died, Charles, I stopped feeling. I stopped hoping for happiness... and then this miracle came along."

John stood gazing at Alice from a distance. Charles could see the bittersweet blend of overwhelming affection for his daughter and heartfelt longing for her mother. Charles reasoned early in the conversation that this story would not have a pleasant ending since John referred to Abby in the past tense. Did she leave? Did she die? Charles could barely contain himself, but knew he again needed to be patient and let his father reveal the details at his own pace.

John walked toward a bookcase and opened a small wooden box that sat on a middle shelf. He pulled out two envelopes, removed the contents and presented them to Charles. "Copies of letters I wrote last year. Easier for you to read them than for me to recount the story." Charles unfolded the first letter.

June 12, 1855
My Very Dear Sir
At the request of my dear wife I write you a few lines.

My Dear Parents

As I expect to be but a few more days to spend in this world I must say farewell! But do not weep or mourn for me. You know the source from whence to draw consolation – In a few more months or years I expect to meet you in another & better world where the wicked cease from troubling & the weary can rest.

I did hope to see you again in this world, but God has ordered it otherwise. He calls and I must go. I have no wish to be here longer, but have rather depart & be with my Savior.

Oh that I could have you here with me that I could have your prayers & your sympathies that are so much needed. May God bless you my Parents & support & comfort you.

My Dear Brother & Sisters

To you I must say farewell. Death is about to take one more of your little band and claim her as his own. Two of our dear sisters have gone & I trust are now hymning the praises of God.

You are all professors of religion. May God enable you to adorn that profession & live a holy & devoted lives. Let the great object of your lives be to do good in the world. My strength fails me. I can say but a few words.[3]

An image of Abby began forming in Charles' mind and he began to see clearly why his father could not bear to recount the loss of this woman. He slowly opened the second letter and began reading, already having difficulty focusing due to the tears welling in his eyes.

August 18, 1855
Contra Costa County California

My Dear Sir
During the long & painful sickness of my dear wife I have continually kept you advised of her condition & I have now to communicate the sad news of her decease. She died last Saturday morning at 5 o'clock. Perfectly calm and resigned and even desirous to depart & with her Savior.

I have been so oppressed with grief that I have not been able to send you the sad intelligence until today & now I can hardly tranquilize myself sufficiently to write.

Yes, my dear Sir your affectionate & and most excellent daughter has departed from the earth to that eternal home where sorrow & sickness are unknown. I have lost the most loving, affectionate & dutiful of wives, & my child the kindest and best of mothers.

Last Sabbath evening the remains were deposited in a place long ago selected by herself in the orchard near the house. The funeral was attended by a minister & a large concourse of friends & neighbors. She was repeatedly visited and consoled by the Rev. Mr. Brierly and other clergymen.

She has for a long time been attended by Mrs. Osgood a member of the Baptist church & a kind & excellent nurse, and by Mrs. Thomson her neighbor & particular friend —

Some months ago she said to me that probably after her death her relatives might desire her body to be sent to the east. I informed her that whatever was her wish it should be complied with – Her reply was that she had no other wish "but to lie by my side of her husband," and whenever it shall please God to my spirit hence it is my intention to have my bones laid by her side.

Your little granddaughter is in good health & is for the present with Mrs. Thomson by the special desires of the mother. A portion of her clothes she desired to be sent to her mother & sisters, & they will be accordingly forwarded in due time – At present I am so overwhelmed with sorrow that I hardly know what to think or determine, but it is probable that within the next six months I shall visit Massachusetts the place of my birth, & bring my little girl to see her grandparents.

I bid you my dear Sir
An affectionate Adieu
John Marsh[4]

Charles sat motionless.

John, Abby, and Alice Marsh[5]

CHAPTER 7

CELESTE AND HARRISON DECIDED to stop at a small café for lunch in Brentwood's quaint old downtown. A few of the buildings were over a hundred years old and added a charm to the area that locals were fighting to retain in the face of rapid development in other parts of the city.

Harrison still preferred going to movies at the two screen cinema downtown, circa nineteen-thirties. He liked the nostalgic feel of the theater, but mostly he was much less likely to run into current or former students, which for most teachers is one of the drawbacks of living in the town where they work.

He already dreaded grocery shopping, knowing that it would likely be a high school student bagging his bottles of wine or six-pack of beer, and saying hi to him as he stood in line wearing shorts, an old t-shirt and flip-flops.

It's not the image that the respected authority figure at the front of the classroom is supposed to portray. Nor is going to see the newest R-rated movie while sitting in front of a group of kids that will be in your classroom on Monday morning. He was already well respected by students, so it wasn't that they would suddenly change their opinion, but it was just easier to avoid the encounters as much as possible.

It was a pleasant spring day, so they decided to eat at a sidewalk table and enjoy the sun. "So what next?" Harrison started.

"Only one other place to go to try to get some answers," Celeste replied matter-of-factly.

Harrison knew what was coming, but asked anyway. "Where's that?"

"His home, of course. We've talked to everyone else but his family. Hopefully they can shed some light on what was going on in Alex's life."

Harrison took a bite of his turkey and Swiss sandwich and didn't quite finish swallowing before asking, "And do you know where they live?"

"Nope, but since he's a student of mine, it's on my computer at the school."

"So," he replied, "I guess I know our next destination."

They arrived at the school parking lot in Harrison's car, deciding to leave Celeste's in the café' parking lot. As they got to the door of her classroom, she broke the silence, "oh crap!"

"What's the matter?" Harrison responded.

"It's the weekend. The alarm is on."

"No worries. I've got the code. We did the science fair a couple weekends back and I needed to be able to turn it off. I don't think they ever change these codes, so it should still work. I'll be right back."

Harrison trotted off toward the main office and within a few minutes, returned. "That should do it. But if the police show up, I'm afraid I'm going to have to claim that you're holding me hostage."

Celeste shot him another one of her glares that Harrison ignored as he strode directly by her into the classroom. He flipped on the lights as Celeste started up the computer.

Within a few minutes she had looked up and written down the address for Alex Moreno's family. "Back toward

52

downtown," she said. "I'll lock up while you go turn the alarms back on."

Harrison did as he was directed and they began the drive to the Moreno home.

"I'm not usually nervous talking to parents," Harrison said as they approached the front door of the home. "But I have to admit, my stomach is churning right now."

The Moreno's lived in an old part of town with small, simple homes framed by mature trees and well used cars and pick-up trucks. Celeste rang the doorbell which was followed immediately by the yapping of a small dog. A few moments later the door was answered by a pleasant looking Hispanic woman about their age.

"Hola," Celeste began. "Hablas inglés?"

"Yes, yes," the women replied, through a thick Mexican accent.

"My name is Celeste Scott and this is Harrison Barrett. We were teachers of Alex. Are you Alex's mom?"

The woman hesitated, apparently registering what was asked, then replied, "Yes, come in, come in."

The two entered the modest Moreno home and Harrison immediately captured the attention of the little dog in the living room which, to Harrison, appeared to be a cross between a small Chihuahua and a large rodent. Mrs. Moreno scooped the dog up and deposited it somewhere in a back room.

"We are so sorry for your loss. Alex was a wonderful young man," Celeste continued. "We are very sad and confused by his death and were just hoping to get some answers. Would you have a few minutes to speak about Alex?"

53

"Of course," Mrs. Moreno replied," as she motioned them to have a seat on the sofa. "Can I get you something to drink?"

"No, thank you," both Harrison and Celeste answered.

Harrison left most of the speaking to Celeste, who periodically interspersed the conversation with Spanish, he assumed, to make Mrs. Moreno feel more comfortable with the two strangers in her home. He scanned the living room, more to give himself something to do than to actually look for anything, in particular.

The room was decorated with bright yellows and reds in a traditional Mexican-American style. Over the mantle hung a large portrait of the Moreno family; mother, father, Alex at about twelve years old, and a younger sister.

To the right of the portrait, a crucifix hung above the back of a recliner; on the wall to the left of the portrait was a framed document of some sort. It looked old to Harrison, with faded ink on yellowed paper. In its center was an image of a bird drawn in a Native American style and surrounded by several small circles of varying sizes. Below the image was writing in a language that he did not recognize.

Mrs. Moreno dabbed at her eyes with a tissue as she and Celeste continued their conversation. Harrison knew that Celeste would not pry too much if it looked as though Alex's mom couldn't handle it. But so far, she seemed perfectly able to talk about him, and almost appeared thankful at times to share some memories.

Harrison got up from the sofa and walked to the family portrait. A happy family, everyone smiling; but he knew that most family photos looked like this, and dark hidden emotions were not usually captured on film. He wondered whether Alex, at this younger age, was already having the same thoughts of depression that he must have had recently.

As Harrison turned to view some smaller pictures that were on an end table, something on the wall grabbed his attention. It was the old framed document. A sudden curiosity overcame him. He moved to view it closer - an old piece of paper with writing on it that was important enough to frame and hang. Harrison's interest was piqued.

The conversation between Celeste and Mrs. Moreno appeared to be winding down. She was as confused as everyone else about why he took his own life. No notes were left behind and she was unaware of any particular troubles he was having. The main thing he worried about was how to pay for college since his father had recently been laid off of work. Otherwise, he seemed happy.

A pause in the conversation gave Harrison an opportunity to speak. "This is a beautiful portrait of your family."

"Thank you," she smiled.

"How old was Alex here?"

"He was thirteen. His sister, Gabriele, was eight. She misses him very much. He was a good big brother and looked out for his little sister."

These remarks started the tears welling in Harrison's eyes so he quickly changed topics.

"This is very interesting," he said, pointing at the framed document. "It looks very old."

"It is very old," Mrs. Moreno replied. "It has been in Alex's father's family for many generations. It was given to Alex's father a year ago by his grandfather shortly before he died in

Mexico. They have always been told it is very, very valuable and must be taken great care of."

"It's wonderful," Harrison replied. "What is it?"

"Nobody really knows. No one in their family knows what it says. They were just told to keep it because it is important."

Harrison smiled at the thought of this little family mystery, though inside he was quite frustrated with not getting a clear answer. The scientist in him was always pushing for direct answers that could be verified with evidence.

"Barre, I think it's time to go," he heard Celeste say. They each gave Mrs. Moreno a hug as they left the house, with no better understanding into Alex's mindset than when they arrived. They talked little on the drive back to the café to pick up Celeste's car, both introspective about their visit to Alex's home; a home that by all evidence was a loving and caring place.

"You OK, C?" Harrison said as he shut the driver's door to her car and knelt down beside it.

"I am, just not sure what to do next."

Harrison was just about to respond when… "Hey Mr. Barrett," came the familiar call from a past or present student that recognized him.

Harrison looked up, slightly annoyed that the intimate moment with Celeste was broken. He knew three of the four students that were cutting through the parking lot in route to unknown activities. "Hi, guys," he said with a smile. "Shouldn't you be doing homework or something?"

"All done," one of the students answered back with a grin as they all exchanged waves.

Harrison returned his attention back to Celeste. "Think about it over the rest of the weekend and we'll talk on Monday at school."

Celeste smiled at him, started her car and drove off.

CHAPTER VIII

September 23, 1856

CHARLES WAS OVERWHELMED with a feeling of contentment. For so many years he searched for his father, trying to reconnect with a distant past. And now here he was, on the other side of the continent with not only his father, but a new sister as well.

John made it clear that he wanted Charles to move into the Great Stone House and the two men arranged to send for the rest of Charles' possessions that were being stored back in Illinois. During the next few months, John hoped to teach his son about the business, beginning with the acquisition of his first cattle.

Being the only physician for miles around, Dr. Marsh could charge just about anything he wanted for his services. His typical rate was one cow per mile that he had to travel to treat the sick or injured. In this way he gradually amassed an impressive herd that could then be bred and slaughtered to feed the growing population in the area; at first mostly Spanish, but as time went on, more and more whites settled in nearby cities such as San Francisco and Martinez.

Even before the discovery of gold, John added sheep, pigs and chickens to his ranch and the demand from miners for fresh meat encouraged him to expand his land holdings even further.

He spent less and less time as a physician as his cattle business grew until presently, the only real doctoring he did was for the Indians living on his land. Charles learned of his father's regular travels to San Francisco, whose population demanded meat and whose large port could ship animals south. John spoke of the art of negotiating deals with the buyers in San Francisco which fascinated Charles, who was naive about this aspect of a business. He was anxious to one day see his father in action, believing this was a skill that needed to be observed to be fully appreciated.

Of particular interest to Charles was the story of his father's encounter with the Bidwell-Bartleson party in 1841; the first wagon train to travel what would become the California trail. John Marsh had been encouraging travelers to venture to the new frontier and was thrilled when the group traversed the Sierra mountain range and arrived at Rancho Los Meganos. He allowed them to butcher a cow in celebration.

John Bidwell, unfortunately, selected Marsh's prized plow oxen. This infuriated Marsh who immediately sent the settlers packing and ran them off his property. After this incident, frequent writings by Bidwell referred to John Marsh as *The Meanest Man in California'* - a title Charles had difficulty accepting based on his recent experience.

FATHER AND SON TOURED the expansive ranch from corner to corner while John discoursed on the details of land use. Which areas were better for cattle and which better for sheep? Why were orchards planted on this parcel and wheat fields on that? What was the current market rate for chicken and price per pound of grapes? Charles soaked it all in and tried his best to ask relevant questions that would impress his father and reassure him that entrusting his son to help with the business was justified.

One constant that Charles could not help but notice during their time together was that, as much as his father seemed to have a great affection for the Indians, he had an equal loathe for the Spanish. He spoke often of the harassment received from Governor Alvarado and his subsequent imprisonment.

He was highly critical of the way the Spanish treated the Indians and suspicious of any business dealings he made with Spanish contacts. Perhaps as a consequence, his communication with the vaqueros was always harsh and direct; and they did not appear to like Dr. Marsh any better, though they kept their feelings well-guarded.

Another particular pleasure for Charles was the time spent with his sister, Alice. He found it remarkable that this child, who lost her mother as he did so many years ago, could still be so full of life. He recalled the years following his own mother's death as being solemn and dark, and it was not until much later in life that he began to understand how to be happy again.

He reasoned that this, of course, must be entirely due to Alice having her father in her life, while he rarely did. It did not make him resentful, but he did wonder how his life might have been different if his father had been around.

Charles took Alice riding on most days, sometimes on horseback and sometimes in a buggy. He felt a renewed sense of purpose for his life as he fed her voracious hunger to learn. They practiced speaking both Spanish and the language of the Miwoks, and Charles was humbled, as well as astonished, at how easy she seemed to pick up the languages. She was definitely her father's daughter.

But perhaps the most interesting aspect of their ventures together was the time spent in the Indian villages. Charles assumed it was due to Alice's unique near-white hair and intense blue eyes that they treated her with such adoration. The women, in particular, would stop working and make a fuss when little Alice came to visit. Children loved to touch her hair and hold her hand and Alice did not seem to mind a bit. Charles sometimes let her play in the village for a while as young boys tried to teach her how to role a hoop with a stick and young girls showed her how to smash acorns with a stone pestle or weave reeds together.

Back at the stone house, father and son spent evenings reading to Alice, alternating whose lap she sat on while one or the other would read bible passages or English poets, finally succumbing to the beckons of Mrs. Thomson trying to put Alice to bed. And after she retired, John typically pulled out cigars and he and Charles spent the rest of the evening smoking and discussing the affairs of the ranch.

LESS THAN A MONTH HAD PASSED since Charles found himself at the doorstep of his father. It was a warm September night and John said good night to Alice and called for Charles to join him in the downstairs study.

Charles was used to their evening chats together, but something sounded different in John's voice this night. As Charles entered the room, his father stood staring out the window, though it was approaching darkness and nothing much could be seen. He also noticed the distinct absence of cigar smoke, which he had become accustomed to when sitting with his father in the evening.

There was a serious tone to John's voice. "Sit, Charles, there is something I must share with you." Charles sat as directed in one of the two wingback chairs in the study. Two oil lamps illuminated the room, one wall mounted and the other a handheld that rested on a wooden end table directly behind a large, leather-bound book that Charles had not noticed before.

"Tomorrow I need to travel to San Francisco," John continued. Hearing this immediately grabbed Charles' attention. Perhaps his father was going to ask Charles to accompany him on a business trip? This is where Charles felt he would really learn about the makings of his father's wealth: the negotiations of sales, the dealings with transportation, and the bargaining for equipment purchases. This is where the true education would be, and he was ready.

"I have business arrangements to make," John began again, still staring out the window. "I'll be riding to Martinez to catch the steamer to San Francisco. Should only be gone a few days."

John finally turned from the window and walked to the end table. The flickering light from the oil lamps highlighted the creases in John's face. For the first time since finding the Great Stone House, Charles was aware of just how old and worn his father was.

John picked up the large book and sat in the adjacent chair. "Charles, what I am about to tell you is known to no other living soul. It was to be shared only with Alice when she was of appropriate age. But you have returned, my son, back from the dead as it were, and I am blessed." Charles watched keenly as his father gripped the leather book. It now seemed clear that this was not just going to be an invitation to a trip.

John dipped his head and now appeared to be contemplating the book, in the same manner he had been gazing out the window moments ago, "I want you to keep this book for me when I am away." John handed it to his son who took it gently, holding it more as if it were made of crystal than paper and leather.

Charles expected to see some hint of emotion on his father's face after hearing this request; some smile or scowl, something to correspond with this action. But there was nothing. His father remained stone-faced, as if one of the rocks composing the wall was perched on John's shoulders.

"What do you mean?" queried Charles.

"That book contains information." John paused again, seeming to search carefully for the right words to use in his description; "….information that is very valuable. If the Spanish had the slightest hint of its existence, they would confiscate it immediately. Every thief and marauder from here to Mexico would be on my land searching… just as pleased to slit my throat for the location as not."

Charles did not understand. What could a book contain that was of such importance that men would kill for it? He could no longer withhold his curiosity as he had done on many previous occasions, waiting for his father to divulge information at his own pace, "What information?" Charles asked, much louder and forcefully than he intended.

"In due time. The book you hold does not contain all of the information, however. I have removed some pages. It is much too risky to have it all in one place."

The aroma from the leather cover was intoxicating. Charles slowly ran his fingers over the scrolled etchings in the leather and the engraved metal brackets binding the pages together and opened the book, anxious to find out what was inside. He became, however, immediately confused. There were words he did not understand and diagrams he could not decipher. He flipped through the pages. More languages; he recognized some Latin and some Spanish, but others he couldn't read at all. Interspersed were letters, or drafts of letters that his father had written, but none appeared to be of significance. More drawings followed.

"I don't understand, Father. Where is the information?"

"Precisely," John replied. "You won't understand. Nor will anyone else... until I explain it to them."

Charles was beginning to figure it out. The various languages. The obscure diagrams. Somewhere imbedded in this book were clues. Clues that must be discovered and then assembled.

"May I assume, Father," Charles finally continued after much consideration, "... that the pages that you removed are important pieces of a puzzle?"

"Quite right. And for now, only I know where those pages are stored. But when I return, Charles, I believe you and I will have much to talk about." And for the first time in their conversation that evening, John showed some emotion as he turned toward his son; the corners of his mouth raised ever so slightly and Charles was sure he detected a twinkle in his father's eye as he said, "Good night, Charles."

Charles slumped back into the chair with the leather-bound book still resting on his lap. "Good night, Father."

The Marsh Family Journal[6]

CHAPTER 9

T HE FINAL BELL OF THE DAY was going to ring in about thirty seconds and the students in Harrison's last period started to pack up their binders, books, and backpacks. Some teachers let their students start preparing to leave with five, or even ten minutes left in the period. But Harrison reasoned that he saw these kids for such a relatively small amount of time during the week that he needed to make the most of every minute, so his students worked from bell to bell.

At the start of a new school year, students tested how early their teachers would let them stop working. However, once they realized that the clock in this classroom did not work... disconnected actually...and found out that Mr. Barrett would confiscate their cell phone if taken out to check the time per school policy, they realized they were at his mercy about when class was over, since virtually no teenagers wore watches anymore.

On this particular day, Harrison was anxious to get them out of his room as soon as possible. He had told Celeste that he would stop by her classroom on the other side of campus just to check on how she was doing. Within a few minutes, he was making his way through the better part of two-thousand adolescents as they ambled off campus.

He always felt that venturing out at this time of the day, so soon after school ended, was a bit like a salmon swimming upstream, but he didn't mind too much since he was one of the staff members that really enjoyed the energy of youth. That energy was one of the reasons he became a teacher in the first place, as life behind a desk or in a lab would seem remarkably dull compared to working at a large high school. The vitality of students was another antidote to the despairs of a single, middle-aged educator.

He entered Celeste's classroom and saw that she was still working with a few students around her desk, so he quietly took a seat in one of the student desks near the back of the room. A few minutes later, the last boy left the room and Celeste joined him in an adjacent seat.

"About a two-point-five for that last kid," Harrison noted nonchalantly.

Celeste knew exactly what Harrison was referring to. Some time ago, he shared with her the theory he had formulated which correlated a student's GPA with the amount that his pants sagged below his waist. Celeste, of course, thought it was ridiculous, but she enjoyed letting him experiment.

The theory was straight forward according to Harrison; for every three inches that a boy's pants sagged below the waistline, he lost one point off his overall GPA. So, a kid whose pants sagged three inches was about a B-average kid; if he sagged six inches, then a C-average. And a kid whose pants were completely below his butt showing off brightly colored boxers or shorts, was not someone who was passing many classes.

And while Celeste laughed at his attempt to quantify his observation, she did appreciate that he actually tried to provide some reasoning. Any boy – of course the theory only worked for boys – that wore his pants so low that he couldn't walk without waddling while clutching them with one hand so they didn't completely fall off, was typically not someone who came from a background where education and academic excellence was emphasized.

In addition, that student's perceived value came from the recognition they got from peers and from their association with certain media, which meant their focus was on socializing, not on academics. Conversely, students that wore pants waist-high likely had academically inclined parents that insisted on it. These students were aware of the negative perception of sagging and so shunned it, concerned more with their achievement than popular culture.

And then, of course, there were all those in between. Harrison knew there were exceptions, but he surprised both Celeste and himself with how accurate he was in his predictions.

Celeste glared at Harrison for a moment, knowing what he wanted her to do, so she humored him. After checking her computer, she returned to where he was sitting and announced, "ha…not even close."

"Well, what is it?"

"Two-point-six-five," Celeste clearly enunciated, which was a reluctant admission that his prediction was pretty accurate…again. Harrison gave a playfully arrogant smirk causing Celeste to just shake her head.

"So, how'd your classes go today?" Harrison began.

"Fair," Celeste replied. "Still having a hard time focusing on work."

"I know what you mean. I…"

"Hi, Miss Scott," came an energetic female voice at the classroom door that had just been flung open. It was Sasha and two other girls whose faces Harrison recognized, but whose names he did not know. "Oh, hi, Mr. B," Sasha bubbled forth when she recognized him sitting in the student desk.

"Hi, girls, what can I do for you?"

"We were wondering if you have some markers we can borrow for a few minutes."

"Sure," Celeste responded as she rose to dig them out of a drawer in the front of the classroom. "What are they for?"

Sasha took the markers and began bounding out of the room. "To make some posters. We got permission to take donations to help out Alex Moreno's family because of what happened last night. Thanks."

"Whoa, whoa, wait a minute, Sasha," Harrison called out. "What happened to Alex's family?"

"Oh my gosh, didn't you hear? They were robbed. Thanks for the pens. We'll bring them back in a few minutes"

Harrison and Celeste shot a stunned look at each other. "Freeze rabbit!" Harrison blurted out. Sasha instantly stopped in her tracks. "More details."

Sasha turned back toward the teachers with the other two girls in tow. "They went to visit a relative out of town and when they got back the next day their house had been broken into."

"Was anything taken?" Harrison inquired.

"I'm not sure. But I know they were already struggling because of paying for Alex's funeral, and now this. That's why we wanted to do something to help."

"Thanks for the info, Sasha. Good luck with the posters and let us know if we can do anything."

"OK, see you in a little bit," Sasha finished as she exited the room, the two other girls still trailing behind.

Harrison and Celeste turned toward each other, both sensing that there was something very disturbing about this. "Are you thinking what I'm thinking?" asked Celeste.

"If you're thinking we need to swing by the Moreno's place again, then yes," answered Harrison.

IT WAS NEARLY FIVE O'CLOCK that afternoon by the time the teachers were able to leave the school and make their way to the Moreno home. Harrison's knock on the door was echoed by the sound of the yapping Chihua-rat on the other side. A moment later, Alex's younger sister, Gabrielle opened the door, one hand on the inside knob, the other on the dog.

"Hi…Gabrielle, right?" Celeste began. "Is your mom home?"

"Just a minute," and the door closed.

Harrison and Celeste stood patiently for several minutes until finally Mrs. Moreno greeted them and invited them inside. Once again, Celeste did most of the talking, first offering her apologies about the break-in and how awful it must be to deal with at this time, and then sympathizing with the feeling of being violated that accompanies such an ordeal. Eventually she finessed the conversation into asking what they went there to find out.

"Was anything taken?"

"A few things," responded Mrs. Moreno. "We don't have much. They took a few dollars, a little bit of jewelry, and the old picture." Mrs. Moreno gestured toward the now bare wall next to the family portrait.

Harrison was surprised he did not notice the missing piece when first entering the room, but he was more disappointed at its loss, knowing that it was a family heirloom and probably irreplaceable. "I'm so sorry," Harrison said, as he finally joined the conversation. "I really liked that picture. In fact I wish I had a copy of it."

"Thank you," responded Mrs. Moreno. "My husband was very sad. We do have copies, but they are not the same."

Harrison became excited at this revelation. "Copies? Really? Would I be able to see one?"

"Of course ... Mija ..." Mrs. Moreno called out. "Gabrielle loves art. She has made many copies of the picture." Gabrielle entered the room, still holding the little dog. It was at that moment that Harrison realized just how much she looked like her brother. The same eyes, nose, and mouth framed by long black hair that was straight rather than short and curly as was Alex's. It again wrenched at his heart knowing that her parents will be reminded of Alex every time they looked at their daughter.

"Mija, go get one of your drawings of the old picture from the wall." Silently, Gabrielle obediently left, only to return a minute later, this time with a large sheet of paper in her hand rather than a dog. She handed it to her mother who passed it on to Harrison.

The paper was larger than the original, but Harrison immediately noticed that the detail of the bird picture in the center appeared exactly like his memory from the previous visit. The lettering of the words seemed to be a perfect copy, as well. "This is very good," he exclaimed, making sure the comment was directed at Gabrielle. "You are a very good artist."

"Thank you," came the meek, but sincere reply.

"I was wondering, would you mind if I borrow this for a little while?"

71

This question caught Celeste's attention as she turned to him quizzically.

"OK," said Gabrielle.

"She has many others," Mrs. Moreno added.

"Thank you. I'll take good care of it. Ready?" Harrison said as he looked toward Celeste.

The two teachers said good-bye and again gave Mrs. Moreno a hug before leaving. As they got into Harrison's car, Celeste could no longer withhold her curiosity. "So what's with the copy of the old picture?"

"Not sure. But there's something intriguing when a home with relatively few valuables gets burglarized and one of the things taken is an old picture that nobody knows anything about."

Harrison started the car and began the drive back to the school parking lot while handing Celeste Gabrielle's drawing to inspect for the first time.

"Well," Celeste said, "I can tell you something else interesting... this writing is in the same language as that journal back at the museum."

Harrison instinctively stepped on the brakes, much harder than he needed to, and the two lurched forward. "Sorry... are you sure?"

"Pretty sure. It looks like the same characters and word structure. And, if Gabrielle drew these accurately, it even looks like the same handwriting."

Various scenarios rattled around in Harrison's head, but none that led to any conclusion so he finally said, "C, I had such a nice time at the museum the other day, I was wondering if you would like to go back with me?"

Celeste looked up from the drawing and into Harrison's eyes. "It's a date."

Harrison felt himself begin to blush. He knew it was not *that* kind of date, but the thought of being on *any* kind of date with Celeste Scott was exhilarating. Staring straight ahead through the windshield, Harrison smiled slightly, "Great.

CHAPTER X

September 24, 1856

THE MORNING WAS CLEAR and warm. In fact, Charles was surprised at how hot the days still were this late into September, a common occurrence for this part of the country. He finished loading a suitcase onto his father's buggy and dabbed a bead of sweat off his forehead. "It's ready, Father," Charles called toward the house.

John held Alice in his arms on the front porch and appeared to whisper something in her ear that made her giggle. Charles was so anxious for his father to return from his trip and tell him more about the leather book, that he hastened his departure with the unrealistic expectation that the sooner he left, the sooner he would return.

John was not originally going to depart until well after lunch, expecting to finish the thirty-mile journey to Martinez just before nightfall and spend the night at Col. Tiff's house. From there he would catch the steamer to San Francisco the following morning.

Charles convinced his father to leave several hours earlier, so he could make it to the Colonel's with plenty of daylight left. It would be safer to travel during that time. Although leaving earlier meant traveling during the hottest part of the day, the temperature would become much more pleasant a short time later with the cool breeze blowing off the delta waters near Martinez.

John finished kissing Alice goodbye and left her holding Mrs. Thomson's hand. As John climbed into the buggy seat and took hold of the reins, Charles could tell that his father's body was aging. The slight groan caused by aching joints was discernible, even from several feet away, and it saddened Charles that they missed so much time together.

"Safe journey, Father."

"Thank you, Charles, see you soon." The vaquero released the horse. John cracked a whip, sending the animal into a slow trot down the trail leading to the west. Charles watched as the buggy parted scattered oak trees in the distance and vanished.

He turned back toward the Great Stone House feeling an unexpected sense of apprehension. With his father out of town, he realized he was in charge of the ranch. And though he knew the position was his for a just a short time, Charles was nervous about the responsibility entrusted to him.

Charles' concern soon passed when he felt a tug on his pant leg. "Can we go to the village?" Alice asked.

"That sounds like a great idea," Charles responded sincerely, thinking that spending time with Alice as she played in the Indian village would put his mind at ease.

JOHN STOPPED SEVERAL TIMES before he even left the outskirts of his property. Once to talk with some Indians tending a vineyard, another time to speak with some vaqueros training horses, and yet again to inspect fencing damaged by squatters at Rancho Los Meganos' western edge. John made a mental note to send someone to make the repair upon his return.

Within a couple of hours, John stopped again, this time in the small town of Antioch on the edge of the San Joaquin River. Some years ago, the town was known as Marsh Landing. Dr. Marsh built a boat dock that could be used to transport his cattle and other supplies up river to Sacramento and Stockton or down river to San Francisco.

After the gold rush increased the town's population dramatically, the new minister convinced the residents to change the name to reference the biblical city of Antioch in order to placate God for the terrible 1851 plague that wiped out most of the town's population.

John did not mind that the town wasn't using his name anymore. In fact, he preferred the anonymity, choosing to lead from behind. He never felt the need to have his name attached to the many causes that he championed or properties that he owned. He continued to call his property Rancho Los Meganos rather than Marsh Ranch, as it was referred to by most locals.

The stop in Antioch was brief, just long enough to check on a business connection and water his horse, before heading on. The next fifteen miles or so followed the banks of the spreading San Joaquin River as it flowed toward Suisun Bay, eventually dumping into the much larger San Pablo Bay before heading out to the Pacific Ocean.

The shores were thickly lined with tules and reeds so the trail to Martinez was some distance from the water. John did not receive as much of a cooling breeze he expected. His aging body was much less tolerant of the rugged journey than in his youth when he could ride for days on buggy or horseback with no ill effects. He felt weary and thankful that the city was just a few miles away now, and Colonel Tiff's house was even closer.

The shadows grew long as Dr. Marsh guided his horse around a bend and into a thicket of large oaks, bordered to the south by a small hill. Though difficult to see, he thought he could make out the figure of a man on horseback on the trail ahead. John had passed several folks on his journey, but this individual appeared to be stopped in the path.

John rarely carried a gun on his journeys, though he regretted not having one now. On his property, his house overflowed with them. He only pulled them out when there was cause, such as chasing off squatters or rounding up rustlers. For the past several years, he didn't even do that since he paid vaqueros to protect his land. John Marsh, however, was not a man to back down from a fight. A life spent on the frontier had hardened him and there were very few men that could take him one-on-one, even at his advancing age.

John was forced to stop his buggy as the man held his ground in the middle of the trail.

"Hola, Señor Marsh," came a voice from the man on the horse.

John did not recognize the voice and with the dimming light, could not see the man's face well. What he did know was that he felt highly irritated that this man would intentionally block his path and slow his journey.

"Kindly move your horse and allow me to pass," John replied with the typical sneer that he used when speaking to most of the Mexicans he encountered.

The man responded in English laced with a Spanish accent so thick that John had to concentrate to understand what he was saying. "You may pass…as soon as you give me the papers."

At this request, John knew immediately there would be trouble. As he held the horse's reins in one hand and the riding whip in the other, he instinctively squeezed his right elbow slowly to his side to reassure himself that his large hunting knife was still nestled under his riding coat.

"I don't know what you're talking about. Now move your horse."

"I don't think so," said the rider as he slowly eased his horse toward the buggy.

The wide brim of a worn hat was covering much of the man's face, but as he moved closer, the gaunt jowls and thick mustache revealed this man to be Felipe, the vaquero from John's ranch. When John recognized him, he became more furious and indignant. "Fuera de mi camino, ya, Felipe!" John barked. But the vaquero did not move.

"Give me the papers." Felipe demanded again, this time much more forcefully.

John carefully examined Felipe's outer garments. There was no indication that he was wearing a gun. If he went for the rifle in the saddle holster, John reasoned he had plenty of time to pull and throw his knife. At this close range, he was sure to be on target.

He was certain that the vaquero had a knife of his own, but he'd be a fool to pull that on John. Every ranch hand was well aware of John's time spent with the Sioux indians where he acquired expert skill in handling a knife. The vaqueros observed this through the years, both in conflict with ranch thieves and in playful demonstrations with the workers.

Again John exclaimed, "I don't have any papers. Now move aside!"

But as he started to lift the whip in an attempt to plow his way through Felipe's horse, he was startled by a hand on the back of the buggy. Someone had run up from behind, grabbed the side of the cart and tried to climb inside. John quickly turned and pushed the man off the side with a force that the intruder clearly did not expect as he tumbled to the ground.

John again lifted the whip, but this time felt his right arm restrained, as a third man leapt onto the seat and grasped John's elbow. John knew the situation was perilous. Three men, any of them could have a gun. He had to escape from here. The Colonel's house was just a mile away; if only he could get there.

John surveyed the scene with the eye of a battle-worn veteran. There was just enough room to the right of the trail to get behind Felipe's horse and around it. He would have to be sure neither of the other two men was on the buggy and Felipe would need to be dismounted for him to have a chance to outrun a single rider on horseback. His mind raced through scenarios – an aggressive attack would be difficult against three individuals.

Surrendering to their demands, however, was not likely to result in a non-violent ending, since a robbery in broad daylight so near town by a man that was recognized meant that these individuals were not planning on leaving any witnesses to testify against them later. No, he needed to catch them off guard; it was the only way to create enough distance to get away.

"Alright. Enough!" John exclaimed as he relaxed the arm that the third man was holding. "The papers you want are in the saddle bag on the floor." he shouted as he nodded toward the back of the buggy.

Felipe guided his horse closer until he was within a few feet of John. He tipped up the wide brim of his hat and squinted through the twilight into the back of the buggy, suspicious of this admission.

"Toss it here," Felipe called in his thick accent, eyeing the third man so that he would release John's arm.

John turned and leaned back, extending his length as he grabbed for the saddlebag. The toss to Felipe was intentionally high and hard and sailed by his horse. As Felipe turned to take notice of where the bag landed, John exploded. With his left hand, he lunged at the man standing on the side of the buggy, grabbed his vest and yanked him forward throwing him off balance. The man flailed his arms trying not to fall and John threw a right fist that connected fully to his jaw, sending him flying backward out of the buggy and toppling to the ground.

As John predicted, the second man began climbing onto the opposite side of the buggy and as he reached in, a thick leather boot caught him directly in the nose. John could tell from past experience that he broke it and the faintly audible snap and stream of blood that immediately began pouring out gave him a momentary sense of satisfaction.

Felipe quickly turned back toward John and starting reaching under his riding coat. John snatched up the whip that had dropped to his side and swung it powerfully across the side of Felipe's face.

The contact twisted Felipe's head as he hollered in pain and John instantly cracked the whip on the tail end of Felipe's horse causing it to buck and dart forward. Felipe's body tumbled off his mount and onto the ground. The next second, the whip cracked again, this time over the top of the buggy horse and it quickly accelerated into a gallop as John raced toward Colonel Tiff's home.

John tried glancing back, but the dust kicked up from the buggy wheels clouded the view. He knew he didn't have much time before they remounted their horses and caught up to him. His muscles tightened and his heart pounded knowing that the house was close; but was it close enough? He neared the end of the long thicket of oak trees. The whip continued to crack, urging his horse faster.

He heard the sound of riders in close pursuit. John discerned that all three must now be on horses. How much farther to the Colonel's?

The buggy rocked violently as it raced across the dirt and rock trail. Someone had caught up. John turned to his left and saw Felipe reaching for the reins of the buggy horse. John swatted at him with the whip but the buggy's speed over the rough terrain jarred so much that he had very little control. With one powerful yank, Felipe pulled the left rein. The horse made a tight veer to the left forcing the buggy to turn much too quickly.

The buggy leaned over, rolling for a moment onto the two right side wheels as John held the reins tightly and shifted his weight. He felt his body lift from the seat as it continued to move in a straight line while the buggy turned and leaned, nearly tumbling over. John's arms thrashed in the air as he grasped for something on which to cling. His body launched from the buggy and plummeted to the ground, his left temple cracking into a large stone.

John, stunned by the impact, could already feel the warmth of blood seeping down the side of his face. He was still conscious, but he knew he was badly hurt. He had to regain control. He had to find his knife.

81

It was too late. The two other men dismounted and pounced. John reached for his knife but it wasn't there. He tried to stand, but the impact to his head made him weak. The men, now at his side, grabbed and lifted him under the arms and John watched Felipe walk toward him.

Through half-open eyes, John saw the broken, bloody nose of one of the men holding him and the red imprint of his fist on the jaw of the other. It was only now that he felt the cool, metal blade of his own knife held against his throat by the man with the broken nose. Though his senses were dulled, John clearly understood the Spanish the man was yelling in his ear as he looked toward Felipe. "Let me kill him now. Look what he did to my face!"

"Not yet," Felipe replied calmly. He pulled out his own knife from under his vest and raised it slowly to John's face. "The bag had only one paper in it. I was told there were more. Where are the others?"

John stared defiantly into Felipe's eyes, but said nothing.

"Where are they?!" Felipe screamed.

John held his gaze.

Felipe turned away, thinking about how to proceed. "Jose, you want to kill him?" Felipe asked the man with the broken nose. Jose nodded.

"...me first."

Felipe whirled back around and thrust his knife into John's chest. The blade instantly punctured a lung and John felt himself losing consciousness as he gasped for breath.

"Charles, please take care of Alice," he whispered.

Felipe withdrew the knife and thrust it again into John's chest. John's eyes closed and again he whispered, faintly, "... please... care for Alice..."

Then slowly, Felipe placed the sharp blade of the knife against John's throat. And with one swift swing of his arm - he slashed.

The two men released their grip and John slumped to the ground. Within seconds, the life completely drained from his body.

Dr. John Marsh was dead ...

Dr. John Marsh[7]

CHAPTER 11

THE PARKING LOT of the Brentwood Historical Museum was empty again when Harrison and Celeste arrived shortly after school ended the following day. Perched exactly where they left her after their first visit, Margaret recognized them as soon as they entered the foyer.

"Hello, and welcome back," Margaret greeted them.

"Thank you," replied Celeste. "Nice to see you again."

"What can I do for you?"

"Well, we were hoping to take a look at that John Marsh journal once again. The one that Alex Moreno was so interested in. Would that be OK?" Harrison asked.

"Of course. Let me get some gloves and I'll take you to the back room."

Harrison spent time observing the museum displays as they waited for Margaret to return. The goldenrod-colored wallpaper stamped in a diamond pattern set a backdrop for an assortment of artifacts: an old wooden end table acted as a display stand for vintage cameras, a crank-type phonograph sat on a china cabinet packed with white porcelain dishware, and in one corner was a desk holding two typewriters.

A small sign read that one was circa 1920 and the other circa 1950. Harrison fondly reminisced for a moment about using an old Smith-Corona typewriter when he was a kid and vividly recalled the difficulty he had moving it from one place to another because of its sheer weight; he was sure it was made of cast iron.

The temptation overcame him and he glanced back to see if Margaret was returning yet, then began clicking the keys of the 1950 version.

"What are you doing?" Celeste chastised quietly.

"Just (click, click, click)…need (click, click)…to (click, click, click)…finish (click, click, ding.)." Harrison smiled subtly, placed his hand on the lever and slid the carriage back to its beginning. "That was great," he sighed. "You know, that's a sensation that our students have never, and probably *will* never, get to experience," he continued, still eyeing longingly at the machine.

Celeste appreciated his admiration for the old device and walked over, put her arm around his shoulder and whispered in his ear. "Just don't break it…"

When they heard Margaret's footsteps approaching, the two quickly turned away from the typewriter as if they were a couple of children guilty of stealing the proverbial cookies.

"Here we go," Margaret said, and she handed them each a pair of disposable gloves and led them to the library room. Apparently, she had already pulled out the large John Marsh leather-bound journal and placed it on the writing desk. "Just let me know when you're finished. I close up at 5:30."

Celeste sat down in the desk chair and unfurled Gabrielle's drawing. Harrison grabbed a chair from another corner of the room and slid it close to Celeste before taking a seat. He opened the journal and began thumbing through the pages, searching for the writing that looked similar to the drawing. About a fourth of the way into the journal, he found some.

"Alright, what do you think? Is it the same language, C?"

"Not only does it look like the same language to me, but I definitely think it was written by the same person. It's the same cursive style. Gabrielle's copy has these big loops on the Y's and the K's just like these phrases in the journal. I would bet that if we had the original, it would fit quite nicely inside this book."

"Pretty wild," replied Harrison.

To Celeste's surprise, he turned and quickly walked out of the room, then reentered a moment later with Margaret. Harrison asked whether she knew what language they were looking at.

"I'm afraid not," she responded. "As I told you before, these artifacts are fairly new to us and our historians have not reviewed them yet. We do know that Dr. Marsh was very adept with languages and spoke many."

"Such as?" Harrison questioned.

"Well, he was knowledgeable in Greek, Latin, Spanish, and several Native American languages."

Harrison continued. "Would you happen to know which Native American languages?"

"I'm not sure anybody knows all of the ones he was familiar with, but I can tell you the one that he knew the best."

Margaret shuffled to the bookcase on the far wall, scanned several of the shelves, then pulled out a thin volume. "This is not the original, of course, but perhaps it will help."

She handed the book to Harrison who read the cover. "*A Translation of the Sioux Language – John Marsh and Marguerite Deconteaux Marsh.*" Harrison anxiously opened the book. The current copyright read 1879, but the original showed as 1830. "Wow." Harrison proclaimed.

Margaret interjected. "John Marsh and his first wife wrote the very first book to translate the language of the Sioux, or Dakota, as some people call them."

Celeste and Harrison looked at each other. "As good a place to start as any," said Celeste.

"Thank you Margaret, we'll take good care of it."

"You're welcome, dear. I'll be in the next room if you need me," and she ambled out.

Harrison again sidled up next to Celeste at the desk and the two browsed through the Sioux dictionary. "This is very cool," said Celeste. "But let's see if it helps. What's the first word on Gabrielle's drawing?"

"*Wikcemna*," responded Harrison.

"Spell it please"

"It looks like w-i-k-c-e-m-n-a"

"Give me a minute. This is arranged by the English word, so I'm going to have to scan through the whole thing to see if there's a.......here it is. *Wikcemna* is the Sioux word for the number 'ten'. This is incredible! Quick, Barre, get some paper and a pen."

It hadn't occurred to either one of them that they might actually translate something, so neither came prepared to write anything down. After a brief moment, Harrison returned to the room with a notepad and pen borrowed from Margaret.

"Alright, I'm ready. The first word is ten. The next word is *akeyamni*; a-k-e-y-a-m-n-i. What does it mean?"

"Hold on, hold on, I'm looking." Celeste flipped through the book running her finger down each page as she searched for the word. "I'm not finding it. I don't see any word spelled like that."

They both got a sudden jolt of disappointed that was exaggerated because it so closely followed their initial enthusiasm. Perhaps that first word was just a lucky coincidence.

On a hunch, Harrison asked, "can you find a listing of numbers?"

"Yes, they're spelled out, but they seem to be here."

"Try scanning through the numbers and see if *akeyamni* shows up."

Harrison waited patiently as Celeste again ran her fingers through the pages. "Got it. You have to put those first two words together. *Wikcemna* by itself means 'ten', but if you put *akeyamni* after it, it means 'thirteen'. Very good, Mr. Barrett."

"I have my moments," Harrison said with a smile. "So the first line is actually thirteen. The next line is a single word alone – *oiyali*; o-i-y-a-l-i."

"Here it is. It means 'steps'."

With this, Harrison and Celeste looked at each other, but said nothing.

"OK, next line has two words – *wiyohpe yata*." Harrison again spelled it carefully for Celeste and she hurriedly searched the book.

"West. It means 'west'."

Harrison straightened up from where he was leaning over Gabrielle's drawing. "So if we did this correctly, this first group of words means 'thirteen steps west'. He turned to Celeste, "you do know what this is starting to sound like…"

"I know what you're thinking, but let's not get ahead of ourselves. First we'll finish the translation, if we can, then we'll try and figure out what it all means. Now what's the next word?"

Harrison read the next word and spelled it out. "s-a-g-l-o-g-a."

"*Sagloga* is another number. It means 'eight'."

"Got it. Hey…this next word looks the same as one we did already…*oiyali*, meaning 'steps'. Look at me…I'm speaking Sioux!" Harrison exclaimed.

Celeste glared at him. "Next?"

"Try this one. Single word. *Itokagata*."

"Found it. Means 'south'. Are you writing all this down?

"Yup, got it. Next is two words – *wikcemna akesakpe*. I bet it's another number."

"Very good – 'sixteen'."

"And the rest of the words in that group I figured out. Another word for 'steps' and for 'west'."

"Alright, Barre, put it all together for me."

Harrison's calm facade disguised an underlying boyish enthusiasm about deciphering part of this old document. He felt like a sleuth, with Celeste as his trusted crime-fighting companion, though he felt she was much prettier than Dr. Watson, or even Robin. Where would these clues lead them? What sort of adventure awaited them?

Celeste snapped him out of his daydream. "Well? What does it all say?"

"Oh…right. Let's see. 'Thirteen steps west. Eight steps south. Sixteen steps west'. Obviously some kind of directions, but from where? To where?"

"I guess that's the big mystery," Celeste replied. "You do realize that more than likely, it's the description for laying out some irrigation ditch or for where to plant an apple tree, or perhaps the location of the latrine."

"Yeah, yeah, I know. But it's intriguing to imagine the possibilities, don't you think?"

"I suppose. What next?"

"No idea. Let's go through the journal and see if there's anything else we can figure out."

Harrison and Celeste spent the rest of the half hour they had left leafing through the John Marsh journal and copying down words they came across that could possibly be Sioux writing. With the museum about to close, they figured they could work on translations later.

They finished making notes on everything they could find. Hearing Margaret scuffling around in the next room, they closed up the book, removed their disposable gloves, and returned the Sioux Translation guide. Margaret was thanked and the pair left the building.

In the parking lot, Harrison leaned one elbow against the roof of Celeste's car. "Do you want to try translating this now or some time later?"

"Of course I'd love to do it now, but we don't have the Sioux Translation guide."

"Uh, Ms. Scott...do you really think that we won't be able to find most, if not all, of this on the Internet?"

Celeste looked at Harrison somewhat embarrassed. "Oh my gosh, I completely forgot about using the web. I think that spending so much time in this old building reading books from the 1800s made me forget what era I was living in."

"No worries. We could sit here and use my iPhone, but it'll be relatively slow and hard to read compared to a computer. If you like, we can stop by my apartment and look this stuff up."

91

Harrison knew that he was treading a fine line asking Celeste to come to his home, especially in the evening. They were friends, of course, but neither had ever been to the other's home at night. He figured, however, that since this was still a school night she might feel comfortable. He was wrong.

"How about we just swing by the school again and use a classroom computer. Custodial staff works late, so we won't have any alarm issues," she said as she smiled coyly at him and got into the driver's seat of her car. "I'll meet you in the staff lot."

Harrison closed her car door.

THEY SAT CLOSE TO EACH OTHER looking at Harrison's classroom computer screen. The words copied from the journal were spread out on a sheet of notepaper on his desk. "I guess there's a couple ways we can try this," Harrison began. "We can just throw a word into Google and see what pops up, or we can try finding a Sioux language site."

"Let's be bold, just Google a word."

"Alright, give me one."

"How about we try one that we already know? Let's do *wakal*. The Marsh Translation Guide said it meant 'upward'."

The two stared intently at the screen as Google listed out options – *(about 102,000 results in 0.14 seconds); a Mexican indie band, Liverpool's premiere computer repair specialist, one of the most water-stressed river basins in India...*

"OK, not helpful," Celeste grunted. "Let's use a translation website. Try Babylon and see if they have something for Sioux. I've used it for variety of languages but never for Native American."

92

On the Babylon website, Harrison noted translation for seventy-five languages, but none of them Sioux.

Getting frustrated, Harrison said, "so…specific words didn't work; general translation site didn't work; how about something in between."

He typed in 'Translation of the Sioux language'. "Bingo. That did it. Translations for Sioux or Dakota or Lakota. All appear to be the same, or at least close to the same. Let's see what we get. W-a-k-a-l." Harrison scanned the computer screen until… "Upward. Excellent. Give me one more word that we had already translated."

"Try *Witoka*, which means a 'male captive'."

A few moments later Harrison responded, "*Witoka* – a captive male. Hmm, I wonder if the Sioux got a lot of use out of this word?"

"Stay focused, Barre. Seems like the site you're using is accurate, so let's translate the rest of this journal."

For the next hour or so, they sorted through the Sioux language website and translated the words copied down from the journal. One of the pages they copied read, *wikcemna akesagloga oiyali wakal*. This was translated into 'eighteen steps upward'.

On a second page were the words, *itokagata inyan titahepiya*. This meant 'south stone wall of house'. And on a third page they found, *ihakab matohota*.

"Well, what does it mean?" Celeste asked as she rushed Harrison to finish searching the site.

"*Ihakab* means 'behind'. And *matohota* means…let's see…here it is… 'grizzly bear'. So it's 'behind the grizzly bear'. . . huh? What's that supposed to mean?"

"That's all of it," Celeste said. "It's getting late. How about we call it a night and try to put it all together tomorrow?"

"Sounds like a plan."

The two shut down the computer, turned off the lights, locked the door to Harrison's classroom and headed back to their cars. As they said good night to each other and drove their separate ways home, the same question simmered in both their minds...*what* was behind the grizzly bear?

CHAPTER XII

September 25, 1856

THE MORNING WAS SURPRISINGLY WARM with only the faintest breeze in the air. The port town of Martinez gradually stirred awake as the merchants and tradesmen took to the streets and buildings near the center of town. In the distance, resting just off the pier, the steam stacks of the San Francisco bound ferry stood tall in the sky.

On the eastern edge of town, a riderless horse and buggy meandered toward the main street. Two or three shopkeepers looked up from their morning rituals and watched as the horse walked by, but it was the county clerk whose curiosity finally persuaded him to make contact and lead it to the nearest hitching post.

Martinez became the county seat soon after the California gold rush, so, unlike many other towns in Contra Costa County or elsewhere in the state, there was a resident lawman. The clerk secured the horse and hurried down the street to report to the sheriff.

Sheriff Nicholas Hunsacker looked much more like an accountant than a frontier lawman. With a thick black beard, balding head, and dressed in a white shirt and dark suit, he appeared much more experienced with reading and writing about law than its enforcement. Nonetheless, the clerk summoned Sheriff Hunsacker from his office just as he sipped his morning coffee.

"Stray horse and buggy wandered into town, sheriff. I figured you oughta take a look at it."

Sheriff Hunsacker stared at the clerk for a moment, pondering whether this was worth the interruption, then, reluctantly decided that he had better investigate. He put on his suit coat and the clerk led him outside to the county building where the horse and buggy were stationed.

It took only a moment for the sheriff to identify the horse's owner. "Pretty obvious by the brand here that this is one of Dr. Marsh's horses."

The seared image of an anchor was unmistakable. For Marsh and many others, the anchor represented profound Christian faith as referenced in Hebrews 6:19 — *This hope we have as an anchor of the soul, a hope both sure and steadfast* ... Marsh also knew its Greek form, *ankura*, a word that resembled *en kurio*, Greek for "in the Lord." The anchor was John Marsh's perfect symbol.

"Where's the rider?"

"That's the strange thing," the clerk responded. "Just the buggy. Nobody was in it when it got into town."

"Do you know if Dr. Marsh was expected today?"

"Don't know, but we can check around."

Within an hour, Sheriff Hunsacker returned to his office with a dozen men that he had assembled, including two of his deputies.

"Gentlemen, we're forming a search party. Dr. Marsh was scheduled to board the ferry to San Francisco this morning and at this time, he has yet to arrive. His horse and buggy made its way into town but there's no sign of him. We'll head east toward his ranch in pairs. Two gunshots means you've found something."

The men mounted their horses and rode out of Martinez along the main trail. They soon dispersed as each pair took a slightly different angle toward the John Marsh ranch. It took less than thirty minutes for the first pair of riders to reach the thick grove of oak trees where they noticed the red-stained soil on the side of the trail. Two shots were fired and a few minutes later the whole search party reunited.

The group moved cautiously toward blood soaked rocks and dirt. Sheriff Hunsacker and several other men dismounted and began to follow drops and splatters. The other men were directed to fan out and search the surrounding area.

John Marsh's body was found in a ditch thirty yards from the trail. The hole in his chest and the gaping slice across his neck made clear the attack's brutality. Hunsacker removed his hat and kneeled next to the body. "Rest in peace, John."

Then, unemotionally, he inspected Marsh's clothes and body. "Took a blow to the head. Bruised knuckles, looks like he put up a fight. Nothing in the pockets, most likely everything stolen. This is interesting…" The sheriff checked the body from head to toe and then intensely examined the boots. "Blood on the boot heel. Must have kicked his attacker, or one of his attackers, probably as they tried to climb into the buggy."

Hunsacker stood up, "Miller," he called to one of the deputies. "I need you to ride out to the Marsh ranch and notify them of what has happened. I hear his son is staying there. Bring him into town."

Deputy Miller immediately mounted his horse and raced off to the east toward Rancho Los Meganos, thoroughly distressed with being assigned the task of breaking the news about John Marsh's death.

Hunsacker sent another man riding back toward town to fetch the undertaker and his wagon. "The rest of you men, pair up and start searching the nearby villages and camps. The doctor's been robbed, so you're looking for anyone possessing something out of the ordinary. Also, anyone with an injury to his face. Looks like the doctor got in a couple good blows. Meet back at my office by sunset."

IT WAS LATE AFTERNOON and the search parties were beginning to return to town. Sheriff Hunsacker and the man he was riding with, a carpenter named Griffin, stopped into the saloon to ease their thirst after riding for hours in the heat and dust.

Several townsfolk sat scattered at tables and a few vaqueros huddled in a corner. The sheriff and the carpenter sipped whiskey for the next thirty minutes or so while they waited for sunset when they would walk the few blocks back to the sheriff's office and meet up with the rest of the search parties.

It was evident to Hunsacker that the vaqueros in the corner had preceded Griffin and himself to the saloon by at least a couple of hours. They were clearly drunk on whiskey and the loud laughter and Spanish conversation could be heard across the room. One of the vaqueros staggered slowly to the bar and in a thick Spanish accent demanded another bottle.

Hunsacker then noticed what he could not see when the man was crouched in the corner; his nose was clearly broken. In fact, it was so broken that Hunsacker couldn't imagine how this man was breathing out of it, as it angled nearly forty-five degrees to the left and showed recent bruising.

Then, oblivious to being watched, the man pulled out a large bundle of money from his vest pocket and placed one of the papers on the counter to pay for his bottle. He stumbled back to the table where he sat with the other two vaqueros, opened the bottle, and poured each another drink.

Hunsacker's mind searched for possible reasons about why this man would have so much money on him. He was a vaquero, after all, certainly making just enough to get by. No way should he have this much money to spare. And then there was the nose. A fresh accident...or something else? There were too many coincidences not to investigate further.

Without the slightest acknowledgement to Griffin standing next to him at the bar, Hunsacker calmly walked across the wooden floor to the corner table where the vaqueros sat. The sheriff was not an imposing figure, fairly short with a round face, so intimidation was typically not his modus operandi. Rather, he talked through most situations whether diffusing potential trouble or gathering information, as he was trying to do here.

He did not recognize any of the men, so he chose not to show his badge, yet, hoping they would not recognize him, either.

"Hola," he said with a smile as he pulled a fourth chair up to the table and straddled it. "Coma esta?"

"Bien," two of them replied.

"And how are you?" the man with the crooked nose asked in his considerable accent.

"Very well. Nothing like a bottle of whiskey to dull your pain," Hunsacker continued as he gulped down the glass that he brought over.

The three vaqueros, feeling amiable in their intoxicated state, lifted their glasses. "No pain." said the one with the

99

crooked nose. They all drank and slammed their shot glasses back onto the table. Hunsacker grabbed up the whiskey bottle and refilled them all, including his own.

"But *you* must feel pain because of your nose. That must have hurt. How did it happen?"

Hunsacker had to concentrate to understand the man's response through the combination of heavy Spanish accent and drunken slur. "No pain now; and the man that did this to me…he has no pain, either."

"Who did that to you?"

"… I can't remember," said the man grinning slightly at his friends.

"When did it happen?"

"Hmm… I can't remember," was the response, still smirking across the table.

Hunsacker decided on a different approach. "I noticed you came into quite a lot of money."

This evoked the type of reaction he was looking for. The grin suddenly washed from the man's face and he turned and glared at the sheriff. Hunsacker met his gaze. The man turned back to his companions. "Vamanos."

The men wobbled as they began getting up. The one with the broken nose reached onto the floor below the table and picked up the saddlebag that was resting there. Hunsacker quickly scanned the scene and abruptly stood up. "Put the bag on the table and raise your hands in the air."

The man now looked thoroughly puzzled. Hunsacker drew back one side of his suit coat to reveal the sheriff's badge. "Put the bag on the table, now!"

The man, still staring into Hunsacker's eyes, complied and laid the bag on the table. There, clearly stamped onto one side, was an anchor, just as it appeared on the horse. Hunsacker slowly opened the other side of his coat to display the firearm he was carrying, being careful not to lose eye contact with the man. "What's your name?"

Again the man paused before responding, "...Jose Olivas."

"Well, Jose Olivas, you and these men . . . are under arrest."

The two other men were visibly surprised by this pronouncement. One of them staggered backward a few feet, slid open his vest to expose a gun, and placed his palm on its handle; but before he could make one more motion, the distinct click of a hammer cocking could be heard to one side.

It was Griffin, who had borrowed the shotgun from behind the bar counter and was now pointing it directly at the man with the gun.

"As I said," continued Hunsacker, "you men are under arrest."

HUNSACKER DECIDED TO LET the three men sleep off their drunken stupor before continuing his questioning of them. The county judge was not likely to consider the information provided by anyone that was intoxicated to be very reliable, and Hunsacker wanted a solid, no doubt-about-it case against the murderer of John Marsh.

During this time he was able to identify the two men that were with Olivas. They both worked at a ranch a few miles outside of town and had spent the past three days preparing cattle for transport. The ranch owner, himself, verified that the two men were on his property and could not have had anything to do with a murder so far away the prior day.

He could not, however, say the same for Olivas, whom he had never seen before. Midway through the day following the arrest, Hunsacker released the two men, convinced they were not involved. His focus was set on Olivas.

Deputy Miller escorted Olivas from the small jail cell in the corner of the sheriff's office to a chair directly across from Hunsacker's desk. Olivas' eyes were blood-shot, his clothes were soiled, and he smelled as though he vomited several times during the night.

Hunsacker settled himself on the other side of the desk and reached for the pen, ink, and paper that he always used to record notes from his interrogations, again giving him the countenance of an accountant rather than a lawman.

The questions were general at first; "When did you get to town? Where were you two days ago? Was anybody with you?" But as the answers were also general and elusive, Hunsacker decided to be much more direct.

"The way I see it, Jose, you're in possession of a large amount of money along with the property belonging to a man that was robbed and murdered. Which is more than enough evidence to hang you. So, if there is anything else you want to say, say it now, because after the rope's around your neck it'll be too late."

Hunsacker could tell that there was more to the story than just this one man robbing and killing one of the most important men in California. The delay in response was long and silent, as Olivas thought through the various scenarios and possible consequences.

Finally, "... it was not me that killed him. I thought that we were just going to rob him. He owed us money from work we did on his ranch last month and he would not pay. I thought we were just going to rob him."

With this admission, the story unfolded, and Hunsacker wrote as fast as he could to keep up with the information provided by Olivas; ...a group of vaqueros who felt that they were owed more money than they were paid. An indignant John Marsh who dismissed their claim in the usual disparaging fashion that he used when dealing with Mexicans. A plan to rob him that took a very different turn when one of their party demanded some sort of paper that the doctor was carrying.

"So, Jose, who was the man that stabbed Dr. Marsh and slit his throat?"

Jose slowly looked up from the floor where he stared continuously since entering the room. "...Moreno. His name is Felipe Moreno."

John Marsh with Miwok and Vaqueros[8]

CHAPTER 13

HARRISON'S MORNING AT WORK began as usual: collecting, reading through, and tossing most of the hard copy mail from his staff box, skimming the e-mail on his classroom computer, and finishing notes on the front board for the first period class.

His mind, however, was far from business as usual. Every other thought was about Alex Moreno, John Marsh, and the mysterious Sioux language. He knew that the distraction affected his teaching, and he knew it wouldn't get any better until he found answers to his questions. Step one, he reasoned, was to learn more about John Marsh.

His preparation period wasn't until after lunch, so he did his best to stay focused until then. Most of his students didn't seem to notice, but two or three made comments wondering whether everything was OK. Sasha, in particular, made a point to come back during lunch to ask what was bothering him. Harrison, of course, knew that anything he said would be immediately reported to the nearest human with a pulse, so he chose to simply smile and assure her that everything was fine.

During his prep period, Harrison put aside the papers he needed to correct and closed the binder that contained the lesson plans he should be working on. Instead, he woke up his computer, went to Google once again, and entered *John Marsh*. In a fraction of a second, Google spat out *about 5,110,000 results (0.09 seconds)*.

Realizing immediately that not every John Marsh was *his* John Marsh, Harrison began to narrow the search. First, *Dr. John*

Marsh. Still more than one. Then, *Dr. John Marsh of 1850s California*. That seemed to do it.

He scanned through the lists of various references and citations until he came across a couple of good historical summaries. Harrison began jotting down notes. *Early life...Born 1799, married to French-Sioux indian mistress - Marguerite Deconteaux. Left Missouri for California on Santa Fe trail in 1835. Got to LA in 1836 and became only doctor in area. Moved north to Rancho Los Meganos in 1837. Became rich from cattle and gold. Married Abby Smith Tucker and had daughter Alice in 1852. Built stone house. Reunited with son Charles who he thought was dead. Sept 24, 1856 was murdered by Felipe Moreno.*

Other details emerged about John Marsh's contributions to the creation of California's statehood, but a different item, one that most people would overlook as seemingly insignificant, caught Harrison's attention. 'Built a stone house.' Something about that seemed familiar, even important, but Harrison could not immediately put a finger on what it was.

With his prep period nearing an end and another thirty-five students about to descend on his classroom, he closed the Internet and reopened the attendance program. A few tweaks needed to be made to the lecture notes on the front board, so he hurriedly added and erased until he was prepared for the start of class.

Right after school was out, Harrison figured he would track down Celeste and they could discuss the information he had found about Marsh. But before he finished planning when and where he would meet her, the bell sounded ending the prior class period and signaling the start of an influx of talkative, energetic teenagers sure to keep his attention for the next ninety minutes.

Harrison called Celeste just before the last bell of the day rang. It was much more likely she would answer the phone at that time, rather than during the moderately controlled chaos of a class leaving their final period. She agreed to swing by his classroom in thirty minutes to chat.

When Celeste arrived at Harrison's room, he was still working with a group of four students at one of the lab stations bordering the side of the classroom. They were all huddled together absorbed in something in the middle of the table.

Celeste cautiously walked over, realizing Harrison was unaware of her entering the room. She learned years ago to be careful when approaching Barre and students at a lab table. On more than one occasion she got an eyeful of something she didn't particularly want to see, usually involving his advanced placement biology students dissecting some poor creature.

Her instincts were right. As she neared the group, she could see between two students that Harrison was probing a large object lying in a tray. She had no desire to watch another frog dissection or dismantling of a cow's eye like she stumbled across earlier in the year.

But the size of this animal, if that's what it was, intensified her curiosity. A few steps closer and she could make out what appeared to be fur. Her eyes surveyed the outline of the animal from in between and around the students as they stared, fixated on whatever it was that Harrison was pointing out to them.

She then caught sight of the specimen's head; though it was upside down, the sharp teeth, pointed ears, and long whiskers were distinct.

"Oh my gosh, Barre, is that a cat?"

The sudden voice from behind startled two of the students so much that they flinched violently. One of the others dropped the scalpel he was using to help Harrison peel back the abdominal skin and point out internal organs.

"Geez, Ms. Scott, you scared the crap out of me." announced one of the alarmed students.

"Oh...sorry, Zach," she responded, remembering his name even though he had her class two years ago. "But really, Mr. Barrett, why on earth do you need to dissect a poor cat?"

Harrison knew where this conversation was going, since he and Celeste debated this topic on more than one occasion in the past, but he decided to accept the bait anyway. "Well, if you must know, these students are doing some extra work prior to taking the advanced placement Biology exam in a couple of weeks and this dissection is a great way to do a summary review on anatomy and physiology."

"But why on a real cat? You know very well that there are some wonderful simulation programs out there that could replace the killing of a cat."

"True, but *we* didn't kill this cat. Besides, do you have any idea how many cats are euthanized each year because they are unwanted?"

"No..."

"Well neither do I ... but it's a lot. So we might as well get some educational value out of them before they get cremated."

Both Harrison and Celeste could tell by the smirks on the student's faces that they were enjoying this bickering between two of their favorite teachers. Recalling why Celeste was there, Harrison decided to bring a quick end to the verbal sparring.

"Anyway, they're just finishing up, so I'll be with you in a minute."

Harrison finished directing the students on the clean-up and storage of the cat carcass, then met Celeste on the side of the classroom furthest from the dissection. Specimen for dissection had not been stored in formaldehyde for years, due to its classification as a carcinogen, but the new preservatives that were currently used for these types of things did not necessarily smell any better, so it often took several days of open doors and windows before the aromatic traces of a cat dissection had dissipated. Harrison tried to spare Celeste any remnants of the odor the best he could.

"So, Barre, what's new?" she began as soon as he sat down across from her.

"I've just been doing a little research on John Marsh and wanted to run it by you to see what you thought."

Harrison showed Celeste his notes, which she reviewed in silence.

"Wow, this is really sad."

"Sad?" Harrison asked. He did not recall reading anything particularly sad...friend of the Sioux Indians, frontier doctor, influential in early California... what was so sad?

"Yes," said Celeste. "He buried two wives. He left a four year-old daughter without a parent. And he was reunited with his long lost son who he actually thought was dead, and within a few weeks was killed. That's tragic."

"Well, when you put it like that, I guess it *is* tragic." Harrison was not surprised that Celeste connected with the humanistic aspect of the story. She was much more likely to feel the emotions of a situation than he was. It was one of the things he admired most about her.

"Anything else jump out at you about the details?"

"Such as?"

"One thing caught my eye, but I'm not quite sure why?"

"What's that?"

"The stone house. According to this, Marsh finished building his great stone house not long before reuniting with his son and then being murdered. I suppose it's interesting to me because I know where that house is."

"You do?" said Celeste with genuine surprise.

"Yeah. It's just on the outskirts of town. You can't see it from the roads, but I went to a fundraiser a few years back that was held on the property surrounding the building. It's really dilapidated now but there is a non-profit group trying to raise money for restoration. In fact, the whole area, house included, is now part of the California State Park system."

"Sounds fascinating. I'd love to see it. I didn't even know it existed."

"Not surprising. It's closed to the public so I don't think most residents in the area know about it, much less have seen it. It is pretty cool, though. The huge walls are all made of stacked, rounded stones, so it's very unusual."

A thoughtful, almost quizzical, look overtook Celeste's face.

"What is it, C?"

"Something you just said. About the stone walls. Do you remember what we translated from the journal? Part of what sounded like directions mentioned something about a stone wall."

"Yes!" shouted Harrison, startling Celeste with his outburst. "That's why it sounded familiar."

"Do you have the translation notes?" she continued.

Harrison quickly trotted to his desk, lifted a few folders that were stacked on one corner, and returned with a manila file folder that contained the details from the Sioux translations. He anxiously flipped through the papers within …and there it was…'eighteen steps upward, south stone wall of house, behind grizzly bear'.

Harrison and Celeste immediately turned and looked at one another without speaking. They knew exactly what each other was thinking. Was it possible that the south stone wall of the house referred to the great stone house that John Marsh built just outside of Brentwood? The one that was still standing, or mostly standing? What could be eighteen steps upward? And how could there be a grizzly bear? The last grizzly in California was killed over 150 years ago.

Harrison broke the silence without losing his gaze at Celeste. "You know there's only one thing we can do…"

"Yup," Celeste replied with a slight mischievous glint in her eyes. "We need to visit an old stone house."

CHAPTER XIV

September 25, 1856

CHARLES ARRIVED IN MARTINEZ in the early evening of the same day his father's body was discovered. He had ridden hard and fast after Deputy Miller relayed the tragedy. The news did not strike Charles as painfully as one might imagine.

Finding his father after so many years still felt surreal, so being without him again so soon and so permanently did not trigger the grief of a typical son losing his father. Though it was difficult for Charles to admit to himself, John Marsh felt more like a business partner than a parent. For now, Charles just felt numb.

The only thing he could focus on was getting to Martinez. The deputy was able to tell him very little about the circumstances surrounding the death, other than it was clearly a murder. And Charles needed to know more…much more.

In the sheriff's office, Charles barged right by the short, round-faced accountant and demanded to see the sheriff. Hunsacker, who was used to being overlooked as a lawman, approached from behind, "That'd be me."

Charles hesitated slightly, expecting, or rather hoping, to see the tall, chiseled dimestore novel gun-slinger sheriff; someone who would travel the face of the earth to track down his father's killer and bring him to justice. Knowing that the disappointment on his face was probably evident, Charles began, "I'm Marsh, Charles Marsh. What happened to my father?"

"Come with me and you can see his body."

Charles was not expecting this to be the first thing out of the sheriff's mouth, but he knew he had to do it sooner or later to get some closure. He had to say good-bye to his father, even if it was only to his lifeless shell.

Hunsacker led the way to the undertaker's during which time neither man said a word. As they entered the back room, Charles inhaled deeply when he saw the outline of a body lying beneath a thin linen sheet. He realized he was physically unable to exhale and hoped he wouldn't pass out.

The undertaker slowly lowered the sheet from above John's head, uncovering just enough to see his face, but not enough to show the severely slashed throat. Charles scanned the face. It was gaunt, but it was the same. The same square jaw and long sideburns. The same weathered, yet distinguished features. It really was his father.

Finally, Charles exhaled slowly, deliberately. It was an exhale that recalled the early years of their life together, when Charles was a young boy and in complete awe of his father; an exhale that expressed the memories of being a lost young man after his father left, spending years searching for both his father *and* himself; an exhale that recounted the joy of being reunited just weeks ago to both a man and a family that seemed to give his life a new purpose and direction. And it was an exhale that expressed a depleted contentment replaced with new uncertainty and doubt.

"How was he killed?"

"Stabbed in the chest. Throat cut," Hunsacker replied matter-of-factly.

With his gaze still fixed on his father's face, Charles asked, "Do you know why?"

"Looks like a robbery by men who used to work for him. From what I was told, could be a dispute over payment for work."

Charles finally turned away from his father's body and looked at Hunsacker directly. "Do you know who did it?"

"We have one man in custody who was involved. Probably not the one who actually killed him, though."

With this, Charles was both relieved and concerned. Quick progress was made in solving this horrific crime, but apparently the culprit was still free. That, in Charles mind, was not acceptable. Charles made a silent pledge to himself, right then and there, that he would do everything he could and would take as long as needed to find and capture his father's murderer.

Hunsacker sensed Charles rising distress. "Let's go back to my office and we can talk."

The sheriff's office was probably the neatest room in all of Martinez. The attention to detail that got Hunsacker elected to the position two years prior was evident in the thoroughly swept wooden floors; the ink, ink pen, and paper were precisely positioned on the large oak desk and the law books and journals were aligned in an orderly fashion on the side bookcase. Even the two jail cells were clean and organized. One might imagine that Hunsacker regularly required the bars be polished.

These details were understandably overlooked by Charles when the men returned to the office. Hunsacker motioned for Charles to have a seat in the cushioned chair opposite his desk and then recounted the information he obtained from Jose Olivas.

"Do you know either of these men...Jose Olivas or Felipe Moreno?"

Charles had seen many of the vaqueros on the ranch, but met very few of them.

"So do you believe this story from Olivas?" questioned Charles.

"At this time, I do," replied Hunsacker. "The part that is most interesting to me and leads me to think that the story is accurate is Olivas' admission that something else was taken from your father; a paper of some sort. We would have no way of knowing this otherwise. Do you have any idea what he might be talking about?"

Charles thought deeply for a few moments. There was his father's journal. The one that he was told was so important. He knew the journal was back at the ranch, but could this paper be part of it?

"No," Charles said. "I can't think of anything."

The two men talked for the next hour about motives, evidence, and the search for Felipe Moreno. Hunsacker made clear in his direct, unemotional manner, that in all likelihood, Moreno was on his way to Mexico.

If he made it, there was nothing they could do. He also emphasized, that his deputies have a very limited range where they could search for this man, but he promised to follow every lead, for as long as he could.

As the conversation ended, Charles felt extremely disturbed by the possibility that his father's killer might get away. He believed that Sheriff Hunsacker would do what he could, but he was worried...very worried, that it wouldn't be enough to bring Felipe Moreno to justice.

EARLY AFTERNOON OF THE following day, Charles arrived back at Rancho Los Meganos. He spent the previous evening arranging for his father's transport to the ranch for burial. He knew his father's wish was to be buried alongside his wife, Abby, under a large oak tree that stood not far from the Great Stone House. John discussed this with Charles in one of the many conversations they had in their short time together and, coincidentally, wrote of his burial wishes in the journal that he shared with Charles prior to leaving for Martinez. Charles would be sure this wish was fulfilled.

By the time Charles finished relaying his father's death to the various staff on the property, it was late in the evening. He talked to the house workers, to the orchard manager, and to the vaquero foreman, being especially careful with the latter not to mention the suspects at this time.

Naturally, the most difficult conversation was with Alice. Sweet, effervescent Alice. How would she take this? What would the consequences be for a young girl to have now lost both parents?

He was grateful that Mrs. Thomson was there, since his life experience interacting with a four-year old consisted of a mere three weeks. Because he wanted to be with Alice if she needed him, he waited to tell her last, at least for this day. Tomorrow, others would be told, including the Indians, to whom his father had become such a friend.

Though Charles was both physically and emotionally exhausted from the prior day's events, he barely slept during the night. Too many images were weaving in and out of his mind: his father's burial, his father's killer, the ranch, little Alice... just as he began focusing on one situation, another would rush forward to clutter his thoughts.

This repeated over and over until he finally noticed the sun beginning to rise through the eastern window. He decided to get up and try to make some progress on something... anything. The logical place to start, he felt, was in his father's study.

JOHN MARSH'S STUDY in the Great Stone House was located on the first floor in the middle of the south wall. In this room, Charles still felt the most connected to his father. It was where they sat and talked for hours, where they read to little Alice, where they smoked cigars together - the aroma still lingering in the fabric. It was also here that John Marsh entrusted his son with his most important document, the meaning of which Charles still did not understand.

The stone walls were concealed by several large bookcases that encased the room entirely except for the door and one window. Each bookcase was stuffed from top to bottom. Charles scanned them completely; books on science, religion, and agriculture; literature in Greek, Latin, English, and Spanish.

Charles even found a dictionary written by his father that translated the Sioux language into English. Other texts were historical in nature and included events from the Roman Empire to the American Revolution. Charles was duly impressed with his father's scholarly depth. He always knew that his father was well read, but this was the first time that he was able to visualize that knowledge.

None of these books was what he was looking for. Fortunately, what he did want, he found quickly. His father's financial ledger was located in the center drawer of the large desk that sat in the center of the room. It was a thickly bound set of documents. It was obvious to Charles that these entries were from only the past two years or so, some of which were inserted after the binding

There were details about purchases and sales, mostly involving cattle. Other lines pertained to equipment purchases to maintain the orchards and payments received for harvested fruit and grains.

On every second or third page were notations about payments to workers including farm-hands, vaqueros, and individuals who transported goods to or from the ranch. Of particular interest to Charles, were the many comments that his father made alongside nearly all of the entries.

Sold   *10 head of cattle to William Smith*
       $20 per head   *$200*
       Fair deal. Smith is a good man to deal with

Purchased   *1 plow horse from MacKenzie in Antioch*
       $35
       Needed another horse quickly for row crops. Probably could have talked him down more

Sold   *50 head of cattle to Sebrian.*
       $25 per head   *$1,250*
       Still a bastard to deal with. Claims that I promised 70 head.

NEARLY TWO HOURS PASSED since Charles started reviewing his father's ledger. The Indian woman who prepared his father's meals brought him breakfast with coffee. He continued sipping, reading, and making mental notes about matters that he thought might be important now or sometime in the future.

As he neared the ledger's last entry, two details caught his eye, so much so that he hurriedly sifted through papers on his father's desk until he found some blank ones and a pen with which to take notes. The first line referenced payment to three vaqueros who were hired to help brand new cattle. The names were Garcia, Moreno, and Olivas.

The names jumped out at Charles like the strike of a startled rattlesnake. Olivas – the man currently held in the county jail for his father's death and Moreno – the man that Olivas identified as being the killer of John Marsh. The comments next to the entry –

Trying to make peace with Sebrian. Hired his son-in-law and two other men to work cattle for two weeks. Not fit for cattle. Injured 2 calves – paid them half.

Here it was – a documented discrepancy about payment. So, the story that Olivas presented to the sheriff had merit. The comments that accompanied a second entry, however, were disturbing...

Have ceased all relations with Sebrian, financial and otherwise. Accusations about cheating son-in-law have grown in intensity.

Claims he'll take it in gold he thinks I have hidden.
Will need to hire more men to secure property boundary.

Charles Marsh[9]

CHAPTER 15

IT WAS THE WEEKEND. Harrison awoke in the early morning to the sound of the neighbor's lawnmower. It did not bother him, however. His mornings were usually filled with the overwhelming silence of living alone - ticking clocks and creaking pipes. The noise of any other life, even too early in the morning, was actually a welcome distraction.

He arranged to pick up Celeste at her Brentwood home at nine in the morning. Their plan was to visit the Old Stone House to 'scope it out'. When he arrived, she answered the doorbell with a bright smile, "I have coffee for us."

"Great," Harrison replied. He was always envious of morning people and Celeste was always particularly perky in the early hours. While most teachers straggled in just prior to their students, she was one of the first to arrive at the school and had an energy that was contagious. She handed him a travel mug with coffee and cream added the way she knew he liked it and breezed by him as they headed toward his car.

It was a clear morning, still cool, but likely to get very warm by afternoon. The drive to the stone house was surprisingly short. It was situated beyond areas of development, but still within the city limits. Harrison took an unmarked road; one with which he was familiar because of his previous visit to the house, but that helped keep its location a relative secret. The last hundred yards or so were not paved and the road terminated at a metal gate.

Another fifty yards beyond the gate, surrounded by large trees and a few scattered shrubs, stood the Great Stone House of

John Marsh, or what was left of it. There were clearly four walls; however, one of them was crumbling. Now propped up with huge wooden beams, the wall looked as if it and the rest of the house could collapse at any moment. Spots where stones were missing speckled the building like battle scars.

Celeste was immediately impressed by the structure's enormity. The sixty-five foot tall tower still took up its position front and center, though it was obvious that it had already undergone some kind of restoration or repair, perhaps many years ago. The top ten feet of the tower appeared to have its stones replaced by wood, which itself was in a state of decay. Yet still it stood, like a weathered and weary sentry on guard after a hundred and fifty years.

"It's incredible. What's the inside like?"

"Don't know. Haven't been in there. When I was here before, they wouldn't let anyone inside because it was unsafe. That was a couple of years ago, but it doesn't look like they've made much progress on the restoration."

"Maybe you didn't donate as much as you could have," said Celeste with a wink.

"Yeah, well sadly, I could donate my entire salary for the year and it still wouldn't be enough to fix up this place... teacher... remember?"

"I remember. So, Mr. Barrett, what's next?"

"How do you feel about hopping fences?"

"Can't say I've had much practice. How about you?"

"More than you might think," Harrison replied with a smirk.

The two walked toward the gate, which appeared to be the lowest and easiest point to scale, since the rest of the fence line was eight feet high.

"Do you need me to help you?" asked Harrison.

"I think I can manage, but I feel like such a criminal for trespassing," she replied as she lowered herself onto the opposite side of the gate

"No worries, it's just a ..."

"Can I help you folks?"

The voice came from behind them and gave Celeste such a start that she inadvertently smacked Harrison in the face with her hand as she quickly released the bar of the gate. The two turned around to see the familiar pale green uniform of a California State Park naturalist.

"Oh...uh...hi," muttered Celeste, feeling once again like a kid up to no good. "We were just admiring the house."

"You two are a little older than most of the teenagers I have to chase out of here."

"Sorry about that," added Harrison. "We were just hoping to get a peek inside. Is there any way to do that?"

"I'm afraid not. The interior of the structure has been off limits for years, ever since the State Park system took it over. Way too unstable for visitors."

"That's too bad," Harrison continued. "It's a great old building. How do you keep the vandals out?"

"Another naturalist or I am here during the day and a caretaker lives nearby who keeps a night watch."

Celeste knew within a second of Harrison asking the question that he wasn't really concerned about vandals.

124

"Well," said Celeste, "I hope the restoration process brings the home back to its former glory. It looks like a wonderful place to visit."

"That's the plan. But we have a long way... and a lot of money... to go. The added challenge is trying to raise money quick before the building totally collapses."

"Good luck with that," Harrison chimed in.

"You folks have a great day," said the naturalist as he secured the gate after releasing Celeste.

Celeste took Harrison's hand and began leading him back toward the car, anxious to escape the embarrassment of being caught climbing over the gate. Half way down the gravel path, Harrison realized he was still holding Celeste's hand; or was she holding his?

At this point, he wasn't sure which. He took notice of her soft skin and firm grip. But he was confused and a little flustered. If he let go now, would she think he didn't want to hold it? Yet, if he held her hand all the way to the car, would she become uncomfortable with him?

The rhythmic crunching of gravel beneath their feet echoed in Harrison's head. He focused on the sound of each step, content to let Celeste determine when to release her hand, which she did when they reached the car.

Harrison again opened the passenger door and carefully closed it behind her. He hoped to see some hint of emotion on Celeste's face as he intentionally walked around the front of the car to the driver's side. But he did not. She appeared lost in her own thoughts and did not look up.

HARRISON DROVE TO A nearby Starbucks where they found a place to sit and talk, neither one feeling the least bit guilty about bringing in their own coffee, since they both felt that in the past few years they spent more than enough money at the coffee house chain to deserve access to the furniture any time they wanted.

Without hesitation Celeste asked, "So when do you want to go?"

"I figure a nighttime caretaker is going to be pretty easy to get by."

"But you heard the naturalist say how unsafe the inside is. You sure you want to risk it?"

"No worries. I'll be in super stealth mode, so not even the house will know I'm there. But I sure don't expect *you* to go."

Celeste glared at him. "You know there's no way I'm missing this."

"Excellent," Harrison smiled. "How about 2 a.m. tonight? I'll bring the flashlights and you bring the directions from the journal."

Celeste raised her coffee mug in a toast. "Another date."

Harrison clinked the thermos Celeste had given him. "Just better leave the high heels at home," he replied.

At about 2:30am, Harrison and Celeste pulled up to the unmarked entrance road leading to the stone house.

"We better walk from here," said Harrison as he pulled onto the shoulder and shut off the engine. It was a cool, still night. The quarter moon gave off just enough light to guide their walk. Fortunately, the road to the fence surrounding the house was easy to follow and they quickly climbed over the gate.

"Well, now we're officially trespassing. How are you doing?" Harrison questioned in a hushed voice.

"It's kind of exciting. But if we get caught, I'll have to say I'm your hostage," Celeste whispered back.

"No problem," smiled Harrison, recalling his same comment when they entered the school the other night.

The two walked cautiously toward the dark image of the house. Celeste was clearly nervous and the eerie noise from scraping branches as trees swayed in the gentle breeze just added to her tension.

"Oh my, God. What is that?" Celeste breathed loudly, leaning in close to Harrison.

Harrison looked up.

Celeste ducked her head onto his shoulder.

Harrison instinctively pulled her close to him and bent down.

The spectral figure flew swiftly and silently directly over their heads. The two watched as it disappeared from view a few yards away behind a tall pine tree. The white ghostlike apparition would have spooked Harrison, too... if not for his biology background.

"Just a barn owl. Probably nesting nearby," he reassured.

As they approached the house, their pace slowed. Finally reaching the large wooden door, they both scanned the façade, more impressed than ever with the sheer enormity of the structure. And now with the moonlight creating a myriad of shadows on the surface of each stone, the walls appeared highly textured, reminding Harrison of the scaled, bumpy skin of a venomous Gila monster.

127

They stared at the door as if it would open like a grocery store's automatic doors. Harrison tugged and pushed on the latch, but to no avail.

"I was afraid that might be a problem. You wait here. I'm going to walk around and see if there is another way in."

Celeste was extremely anxious about being left alone in this situation, but she agreed. On the side of the house that was crumbling, Harrison saw two boarded up windows that looked low enough to the ground to climb through. He opened the fanny-pack he was wearing and removed a large screwdriver. It only took a few moments to pry one side of the wooden planks back enough for him to hoist his body onto and over the window sill.

Once inside, Harrison took out a flashlight. The interior was otherwise pitch black and Harrison dare not move until he could see where he was going. The floor was covered with wooden planks and he eased over them in the direction of the front door. Unlatching the lock, he carefully swung it open.

"Well hello, darling...won't you come in?" he said with his best Cary Grant impression, trying to put Celeste at ease.

Celeste responded with her own interpretation of a 40's era starlet. "Well thank you, Mr. Barrett. Such a beautiful home you have here. Won't you be a dear and fetch me champagne?"

Harrison handed her another flashlight from his fanny-pack. Celeste unfolded the paper with directions translated from the journal and illuminated it.

"So here we go, Barre. Time to find out if this stuff means anything. *Eighteen steps upward.*"

"There's only one place in here that has eighteen steps upward, and that's the tower."

With flashlights shining and Celeste clinging to Harrison's arm, they walked gingerly toward the tower to the left of the front door. Each squeaking step sounded like a wailing banshee against the backdrop of the night's silence. Harrison thought for sure that if a caretaker were awake nearby, there was no way he wouldn't hear them.

When they got to the bottom of the tower, they were once again captivated by its magnitude, in both height and width. In the focused beam of their flashlights, they could make out the wooden stairs spiraling upward.

"You do realize, Barre, that those wooden stairs are over a hundred and fifty years old."

"Yeah, I was thinkin' the same thing . . . you wanna go first?"

Celeste glared at him.

"OK, OK. Wish me luck."

"Good luck. Oh, and don't forget to count."

Harrison's muscles tensed as he began slowly ascending the stairs, carefully testing the fortitude of each step before putting his full weight on it.

"6...7..." she heard him whisper.

Celeste lost sight of him as he followed the winding path of the staircase upward into the tower.

"8...9..."

THE SOUND OF CRACKING WOOD echoed through house.

Harrison cried out!

A rush of fear shot through Celeste.

"Barre? Barre?!" she shouted, oblivious to the possibility of arousing the caretaker.

There was silence.

"Barre? What happened?" she again yelled, desperate for a response.

Finally a reply. "Number 10. I don't recommend stepping on stair number 10. The rest seem stable. I'm at stair 18 now. You want to come up?"

Harrison didn't realize that Celeste had already started climbing, so he was surprised by how quickly she met up with him. All four walls of the tower were made of the same rounded stones that comprised the rest of the house and both Harrison and Celeste felt obliged to rest one hand on a stone due to the unrealistic assumption that if the precarious staircase came crashing down they'd be able to hang onto the wall.

"So, what's next?

"*South stone wall of house.* Do you know which way is south?"

"I will in a minute." Harrison reached back into his fanny-pack and pulled out a compass. "That way is north, so this way is south," he said, pointing to the wall directly behind him.

"Watch out!"

Celeste screamed and lunged into Harrison's arms.

Harrison ducked and dipped Celeste down with him.

Celeste's heart again raced with fright.

"What?! What is it?!"

Harrison paused, scanning the darkness above him. "Bats," he said calmly. "Probably California Myotis, though it's hard to tell when they're moving so fast."

130

He could feel the tension release from Celeste's body as she stood upright. "Don't feel bad," Harrison continued, "they startled me too."

Celeste, realizing that she was still tightly clenching Harrison's hand, slowly let go. "I don't know how much more of this I can take."

I hear you. If we don't find anything soon, we'll get out of here."

"Great. So the last line says *behind grizzly bear*. Would you mind showing me where the grizzly bear is? Because if there is a grizzly bear in here with us, I'd really like to leave now."

"Yeah, I'm a little confused about that one, too. Take a look at this wall with me. Maybe it's a picture or drawing of some sort."

Celeste squeezed onto the same step as Harrison. They examined the wall for twenty minutes, moving their flashlights back and forth, up and down over the stones, searching for some faint painting or etching that could be perceived as a bear. There was nothing.

Frustrated, Harrison carefully sat down on the twentieth stair, his feet still resting on the eighteenth. "I guess we always figured it was unlikely we'd find anything."

Celeste, who was still standing on the eighteenth, tried to console him. "Maybe we're just missing some other clue. Why would it be a grizzly bear, anyway? You said they were becoming rare in California during Marsh's time, right? So what's the difference between a grizzly bear and any other bear?"

"Well you'd definitely notice the difference if you saw them side by side, since the grizzly is much bigger than most other bears, especially the common black bears. But if you just saw a bear wandering around the forest, one of the ways to tell is that the grizzlies have a really high shoulder, almost like a hump. Most of the drawings that you see done of bears by Native Americans are of grizzlies and you can tell because of the outline of the big shoulder hump."

"Kind of like that?"

Harrison looked up at Celeste who was pointing at the south wall. He didn't see anything on the wall and squinted intensely in the light of his flashlight trying to make out what she was pointing at. "Uh, I don't see anything on the wall."

"Not *on* the wall, silly, *the* wall."

Harrison was still perplexed until, as if someone just shook him awake, he saw it. Five feet above the eighteenth step was the perfect outline of a grizzly bear. Not *on* a stone, it *was* a stone. The rounded stones of which the whole house was composed were irregular shaped. But this one was very different.

"You're brilliant." he exclaimed.

"Don't get too excited. It's just a rock. Could be a coincidence."

"Well, one way to find out." Harrison reached back into his fanny-pack and pulled out the large screwdriver and a hammer.

"Very impressive, Inspector Gadget," Celeste smirked.

"Ex-boy scout," Harrison responded.

Harrison began chipping away at the mortar surrounding the bear-shaped stone.

"Can't you do that any quieter?" Celeste chastised. "You're going to wake the caretaker."

"Sure, as soon as you find me a styrofoam mallet and chisel that can break through mortar and stone, I'd be happy to use them."

Harrison continued pounding and prying for the next several minutes until the stone was loose enough for him to wedge the screwdriver behind and completely remove. He switched out the hammer for his flashlight and bent down, shining it into the vacated space in the wall. Celeste hovered eagerly directly behind him.

"Oh my God."

"What?" Celeste exclaimed.

"Do you realize that I just vandalized a historic building?"

Celeste smacked him playfully on the shoulder. "Yeah, you and me both. Now hurry up before someone comes. Is there anything interesting behind there?"

"Well, it depends."

"On what?"

"On whether this piece paper back here has anything interesting on it."

Harrison reached into the opening and pulled out a rolled up paper, perhaps eight inches wide, looking very aged and weathered. He looked at Celeste and Celeste looked at him. Giddy grins spread across their faces.

"I can't believe it." exclaimed Celeste.

"Me neither. Come on; let's get out of here and off these rickety steps. We can head back to my place and open it up."

CHAPTER XVI

THE FOLLOWING DAY, Charles left the house early to catch up with the ranch foreman. He spent the prior day reviewing financial records and various correspondence found within his father's study of the Great Stone House.

He wrote notes to himself about details he felt were important and questions that needed further clarification. He was still very unsure whether he could manage the huge ranch, but there was at least some sense of relief, as small as it was, that he had made progress.

His mind was cluttered with questions to ask and directions to give. But the one subject that he most needed to resolve was his father's murder. He wanted more information about Felipe Moreno. Who was he? What did he do on the ranch? Where did he go after the murder? And who is this Sebrian fellow, the one with who his father had a heated dispute? The foreman was as good a place to start as any to get answers.

The outlying ranch buildings were already bustling with activity when Charles arrived on horseback. Vaqueros readied their own horses and equipment to move the largest herd of cattle from their current location in the distant foothills to an adjacent range that provided better grazing.

The foreman met Charles in the small wooden building that served as an office. His name was James Whitman, but to most workers he was 'Mr. Whit'. Charles heard his father call him just 'Whit', so that's how he referred to him.

They met previously, but never engaged in much conversation since the interaction was always between Whit and his father. Whit was probably in his forties, but his weather-worn skin, tan and leathery from a lifetime of exposure to the elements, made him look much older. The thick, bushy mustache covered so much of his lips that it was difficult to see his mouth move when he talked.

Whit offered a chair and some coffee and again expressed his condolences, as he had a couple of days prior when Charles first relayed details about his father's death.

The two men talked for a while about affairs of the ranch, mostly involving Charles asking questions and Whit answering. The one directive that Charles gave was to go forward with the sale of two dozen cattle to a ranch down south. Fortunately, no other business decisions were currently needed, but Charles knew they were coming.

When the conversation about ranch management wound down, Charles began with the real issues gnawing at him. "What can you tell me about Jose Olivas, Felipe Moreno, and Juan Garcia?"

"Well, let's see," Whit began, with a voice that sounded as gravelly as he appeared. "Those were the three fellas that Dr. Marsh asked me to bring on a few months back. Didn't work here for long since none of them had much cattle experience. Garcia was quiet, probably the best worker. Olivas and Moreno talked more than they worked. Neither knew what the hell they were doing with a cow."

"So why did my father ask you to take them on?"

"Moreno was the son-in-law of Ygnacio Sebrian, the fella that owns the ranch on the next parcel over, about ten miles to the south."

The man suspected of killing his father was related to the man with whom his father was in a conflict? This, Charles felt, was an important association; one that he needed to know more about.

"Your father had problems with Sebrian for years, bickering about property lines and such. Finally, he tried to help make peace by hiring Moreno, but it didn't work out. And the one thing Doc Marsh would never do is pay a man who didn't earn it. Things got worse after that. Heard that Sebrian even threatened Doc Marsh."

"My father's notes mentioned that Sebrian also warned that he would get the money by taking it from the hidden gold. Any idea what he was talking about?"

"Shoot, that story's been around for years. People been saying Doc Marsh had thousands of dollars in gold hidden somewhere on his property. Ain't no truth to it, though. If anything were buried on this land, someone would've come across it by now."

Charles and Whit talked for a short time more before Charles recognized that the foreman needed to get out into the hills to supervise the movement of the cattle. He reassured Whit that he would do the best he could to keep the ranch running as smoothly as his father did. Whit agreed to assist however he could. Mostly, Charles knew, that would mean answering a lot more questions.

As Charles mounted his horse for the ride back to the house, he had already planned out the next step in the search for

136

his father's killer. While obvious, the outcome was uncertain – he had to meet Ygnacio Sebrian.

THE TRAIL TOWARD THE SOUTH of Rancho Los Meganos was pleasant, and Charles enjoyed the cool breeze on his face complimented by the choir of early morning birds and the scent of tall grasses. Even the smell of cattle was starting to grow on him. His external senses were in stark contrast to the unpleasant churning inside his stomach at the thought of confronting Ygnacio Sebrian. He knew nothing about this man or how much he may have hated his father.

The path led to a gate at the fence line that he assumed was the boundary between the Marsh and Sebrian properties. Charles passed through and continued a slow trot for another mile or two until he saw a small complex of buildings perched on a low hill.

As he got closer, he could make out sheds and a stable surrounding a large wood-framed house; and while the house was large in comparison to most residences, it was extremely modest when likened to John Marsh's Great Stone House, but then, virtually every building west of the Mississippi was modest in comparison.

Charles directed his horse toward the front of the home. He saw workers attending to animals in the stable and others doing household chores. As he neared, a vaquero rode out to meet him. "Hola, Señor. Can I help you with something?"

The Spanish accent was heavy, but easily understandable. "Yes, my name is Charles Marsh. I would like to speak with Ygnacio Sebrian. Is this his place?"

The vaquero cocked his head to the side and paused, as if both translating the words and examining the man. "Wait here, Señor."

The man rode back to the house, dismounted and entered. Several minutes later, he reappeared at the front door and motioned for Charles to approach. Charles dismounted and a second vaquero came and led his horse to a hitching post while Charles ascended the front steps and entered the home.

It was not as he expected. The interior of the home was bright and colorful. Red and gold blankets and rugs were spread throughout the main living area. Mexican vases in terracotta and yellows filled corners and vibrant paintings of horses and landscapes decorated the walls. It was warm and cheerful.

Charles was escorted to a chair upholstered in more brightly colored fabrics. He sat for nearly ten minutes before finally hearing a rear door to the house open and close and the sound of boot steps striking the planks of the wooden floor at a rapid pace.

A man approached, removed the wide-brimmed hat of a traditional vaquero and flung it to the side. He stopped a few feet from where Charles was seated, reached out his hand, and with a smile said, "Hola, Señor Marsh. I am Ygnacio Sebrian. I have been expecting you."

Several things about this initial encounter confounded Charles. Why was the owner of this large property dressed like a ranch hand – his father would never do so? Why was he expected – he did not tell anyone he was coming here? And why, with such a heated rivalry with his father, was this man smiling?

Charles rose from his chair to shake Sebrian's hand and was again somewhat surprised as he, being just under six feet tall, seemed to tower over Sebrian, who couldn't be more than five feet five inches in height. Not the image Charles pictured of the man with whom his father would have had such a bitter rivalry.

"Please, sit. We have much to talk about."

Charles sat back down and Sebrian joined him in an adjacent chair. He shouted something in Spanish that Charles did not understand and immediately a woman entered the room with a tray carrying a whiskey bottle and glasses. Sebrian poured the whiskey and handed a glass to Charles.

"Let us drink to your father."

Charles was not used to drinking whiskey this early in the day, but did not want to be disrespectful. "To my father." They hoisted the liquor-filled shot glasses and gulped them down. Sebrian offered another drink.

"No, thank you. I am fine."

"Your father and I disagreed on many things, but he was a good business man. Very impressive," Sebrian continued. "He accomplished many great things. I am sorry for your loss."

"Thank you."

"Now, you are here because you must have some questions for me."

Charles was still bewildered about how Sebrian knew that he wanted to talk to him. "Well, yes, I do. My understanding is that you and my father did not get along, and that you even threatened him."

"Señor Marsh, people say many things in the heat of an argument. It does not mean that they will do them."

"What can you tell me about Felipe Moreno? I understand that he is your son-in-law."

"Ah, yes. Now we come to the real reason you are here. Felipe is married to my daughter, Isabella. Not the man I would have chosen for her, but they were in love so I did not prevent their marriage. Your father gave him a job a few months ago, but did not pay him as promised. This was one of the disagreements that we had. If you promise to pay a man, you should pay him."

"So where is Felipe now?"

"That, Señor Marsh, I do not know. I have not seen him since your father died."

"Is that a coincidence?"

"Perhaps. Perhaps not. I know that you are looking for him because you believe that he had something to do with killing your father. I cannot say whether he did or did not. But I can tell you that I am also looking for him. He has not been to see my daughter since before the murder and she does not know where he is either. So, you see, we both have a common goal."

Again, Charles had not anticipated that the conversation would take this direction. It appeared that Sebrian, at least for now, would be no help in tracking down Moreno. But Charles knew that he could not leave without asking one more question.

"What can you tell me about gold that my father supposedly has hidden?"

The change in Sebrian's demeanor was subtle but discernible to Charles; a brief hesitation in his motion, a slight downturn in the perpetual smile that he had displayed since entering the room, and a mild clenching of his jaw, all indicated to Charles that this topic had more significance for Sebrian.

"Señor Marsh, people have been telling that story for years. Only a fool would hide money where it could be found rather than keep it in the bank. Your father was no fool."

No, thought Charles, he was no fool, but he also did not trust people *or* institutions. To him, most were incompetent or dishonest. Could it actually be possible that his father *did* keep his money on his property rather than in a bank perhaps in San Francisco? The notion seemed preposterous; nonetheless, Charles needed to learn more.

The two men exchanged goodbyes and Charles began the ride back to the Great Stone House. He was still confused by the cordial meeting with Sebrian and intrigued by the story of gold. But if he could conclude anything, it was that no matter what the cost and no matter how long it took – he had to find Felipe Moreno.

CHAPTER 17

HARRISON TUCKED THE PAPER into his fanny-pack and the two began delicately descending the staircase.

"Stop. What was that?" Celeste whispered.

The sound emanating from the room below was the now familiar squeaking of the weary floorboards.

"Oh, crap," Harrison whispered back. "Must be the caretaker."

"What do you want to do?"

"Turn off the flashlights and be still. We'll see if he knows we're here."

The methodical steps grew louder and closer to Harrison and Celeste's perch, halfway up the staircase.

Again Celeste's heart began racing.

Then the footsteps seemed to grow fainter.

Celeste eased the clench she had on Harrison's arm as she started to relax. Harrison mimed the wiping of his brow in relief.

Then the squeaking stopped…

Harrison could tell Celeste was holding her breath, just as he was. He wondered to himself which of the two would have to breathe first. It turned out it didn't matter.

"Come down, now!" shouted a man with a heavy accent.

Harrison leaned over Celeste's shoulder while she stood a step below him. "I guess that answers that question."

When they reached the bottom of the stairs, they were greeted by a bright light shining in their eyes, blinding them from viewing the man before them. Both Harrison and Celeste returned the glare with their own flashlights but all they could make out was a silhouette and curly dark hair.

Harrison began, "well, I guess you're wondering why ..."

"Shut up." the man interrupted in his thick accent.

Harrison and Celeste were taken aback and their somewhat light-hearted attitude changed abruptly. Celeste decided to try her explanation. "We're sorry for trespassing, we just wanted ..."

"I said shut up! Now give me the map."

At this point, Harrison and Celeste were perplexed and their anxiety level increased dramatically. This is not what they expected from a caretaker ... and what map?

"I'm not sure what you're talking about," responded Harrison.

"You found the map. You will give it to me now."

Harrison felt an immediate need to try and diffuse the situation. The man was about ten feet away, so he began walking toward him to get a better look at who he was dealing with. "Listen, can we go outside and talk about this?"

Before Harrison could get near enough to get a good look, the man quickly reached behind his back and in the next instant Harrison's flashlight was reflecting off of the barrel of a small caliber hand gun.

He froze, immediately recalculating the severity of the situation. This individual was definitely not the caretaker hired by the State Parks to monitor vandalism by teenagers. But who was he? How did he know they were there? And how did he know that they found something?

What started as an investigation into why a boy would kill himself, had led them to an isolated stone house with a man pointing a gun at them. There was something much more intriguing going on here – and something much more dangerous.

Celeste saw the man pull the gun and reacted instinctively by again trying to calm the situation. She had not yet deduced that this man was not just an overzealous caretaker. She walked quickly toward him. "Please, sir, if you let us explain…"

But when she got within a few feet, the man lunged. His flashlight struck her in the head! The shock of the contact and force of the blow caused her to lose balance and tumble to the floor.

Harrison was stunned. He quickly bent down to help Celeste and as he stood back up, a feeling rage rose as well.

"Looks like I'll just have to take it…" said the man, whose accent now took on a sinister tone.

Harrison stood just a few feet away from the curly-haired man, a gun pointed at his chest. Both men still had flashlights shining in the eyes of one another. Harrison's martial arts training from years past taught him how to disarm and incapacitate a man in this situation and he had practiced it many times when he was younger. But that was years ago and it was never the same as real life. He concluded that it was unlikely this man would let the two of them out of the house alive, even if he did give up the map, or whatever it was.

He assessed their precarious situation. First, he needed a distraction to get the man's eyes to shift away from them. Then a two hand wrist grab to be sure to get control of the weapon. Celeste was already standing to his right, away from the gun in case it went off, so that was good. Then, with the man in close, an elbow strike to the face to disorient, followed by a side kick to the kneecap to disable. With some luck, he and Celeste would be able to escape.

Click. It was the clearly audible sound made by the handgun's hammer cocking.

Harrison exploded! He tossed his flashlight to his left. While it was still in the air he leapt forward and grabbed the man's gun and wrist with both hands, twisting them backward. He could feel the gun releasing from the man's hand, but he didn't have full control and it dropped to the floor.

In another instant, he pulled the man's arm in close to his body and smashed an elbow to his face, making contact with his mouth. The man, clearly stunned by the sudden attack, staggered back. Harrison then rotated to his left and launched a side kick that made direct impact to the man's knee, causing him to shout with pain and collapse to the ground.

Harrison thought about searching for the gun, but it was dark and he no longer had his flashlight. He immediately spun back around the other direction, grabbed Celeste's hand and pulled her toward the door.

Celeste was still dazed from the blow to her head, but she ran alongside Harrison out the front door, over the gate, down the path to the street, and into Harrison's car. He sped down the road toward his house, not confident of their escape until they saw the familiar city lights.

"I'm taking you to the hospital."

"No, no," Celeste replied, rubbing her head. "It's just a little bump. I'm fine."

"Are you sure? Better safe than sorry."

"Yes, I'm sure. Thanks. By the way… what the hell just happened back there?"

"I'm not exactly sure. But I do know we need to get the police involved."

"No kidding. Only ..."

"What?"

"Well, if we go to the police right now they're going to confiscate the paper we found before we can even look at it."

"Good point. What did you have in mind?"

"How about this ... take me home so I can patch up my bruise and get some rest, then pick me up tomorrow morning and we'll head down to the police station together. By then, you'll have had a chance to examine it."

"Sounds good. But are you sure your head is ok?"

"I'm sure. I just need to lie down for a bit. You should know by now how hard-headed I am."

Celeste smiled at Harrison and he smiled back. It was a welcome release from the tension of the events they just experienced. "Call me when you're up and ready to go. This time *I'll* bring the coffee."

THE MORNING CAME QUICKLY. Harrison received Celeste's call and met her at her doorway with the caramel macchiato that he picked up on his way over. It was now around 9 a.m. on Sunday and the roads were empty except for those heading toward an early church service.

"Get any sleep last night?" he asked.

"Not much. By the way, thanks for getting us out of that jam last night. I don't know what would've happened if you didn't do what you did. That was really brave."

Harrison felt the rush of blood to his face that was common when he blushed. "Uh ... thanks. More luck than anything else. I'm just glad you're OK. Anyway ..." Harrison quickly tried to change the subject. "I got a chance to look at the paper."

After the previous night's trauma, the whole reason for visiting the Old Stone House slipped Celeste's mind. "Oh my gosh. I totally forgot. So what is it?"

Harrison reached into his fanny-pack, which was now resting between the driver and passenger seats, and took out the paper. It was rolled up the same way they found it behind the bear-shaped stone. "It's hard to explain. Take a look."

Celeste took the paper, carefully untied the twine that bound it, and slowly unrolled it. "Ok, I'm looking and I still don't know what it is."

"I told you it was hard to explain."

The only marking on the paper was a large triangle with irregular sides. At the corner of each side were words that appeared to be Latin, or perhaps Greek, mixed with other words that looked more Native American.

"Well if this is a map, like the man with the gun said, we're going to need some help making sense of it," Celeste continued.

They arrived at the police station located near the historic downtown. Harrison pulled into a parking space, turned off the car, and turned to Celeste. "Alright, Public Enemy Number One, you ready to turn yourself in?"

"What happened last night was too serious not to report. And by the way, it's nice you think I'm number one..." She beamed at Harrison.

Harrison again sensed an oncoming blush so he quickly exited the car.

Inside the police station, they were greeted by a receptionist who led them to a patrol officer to take a report. They recounted the events while the officer, a rather young looking twenty-something, took notes. He eased their fears about the possibility of arrest for breaking and entering the Old Stone House.

"Nothing," he explained, "has been reported, so we won't consider it a crime at this time. What I will have to do though, is turn it over to one of the detectives to follow up with this paper that you found and then see if we can figure out who the man was that attacked you. You're right that it wasn't the caretaker out there; he's Caucasian and about seventy-five years old."

"No detectives are on duty today, so expect that someone will contact you tomorrow. Since you're both Brentwood High teachers, maybe he can meet you at the school after work."

"That should be fine," Celeste responded, not waiting for Harrison's opinion.

"What about the paper we found…the map, or whatever it is?" Harrison quickly added.

"Now that, of course, will need to stay here until we can figure out its rightful owner."

"I was afraid of that. So are we free to go, now?"

"Sure. Enjoy the rest of your weekend."

"Thanks," they replied in unison.

Back outside in the parking lot, Celeste paused before getting into Harrison's car. "So, Barre, now what? The police have the map, or whatever it is, and it doesn't look like we're going to be getting it back. I don't suppose you made a copy, did you?"

"No, I didn't," he said dejectedly.

Just before Harrison closed the car door that he again held open for Celeste, he continued nonchalantly, "...but I did scan it"

CHAPTER XVIII

December 20, 1856

THREE MONTHS HAD PASSED since the John Marsh murder. Charles spent his time learning about and looking after Rancho Los Meganos' affairs. He had discussions with ranch personnel, met with the Indians that continued to work the crops, and made the occasional trip to Martinez to meet with buyers and sellers.

Nevertheless, with each day that passed, his restlessness grew more profound. Sheriff Hunsacker kept in communication with Charles, just as he said he would, but as Charles feared, no progress had been made in locating Felipe Moreno. Each time he was in Martinez, Charles had long meetings with Hunsacker. Jose Olivas signed a written confession regarding the incidents that took place on the evening of September 24, 1856 in exchange for a reduced sentence. Moreno was named the killer.

The wanted posters were placed around the county soon after the murder, so Moreno's face was sure to be recognized if he was in the area. The reward began at $250, was then upped to $500, and now showed $1,000. Surely if someone saw him, they would turn him in for that amount of money.

Hunsacker insisted he was doing everything he could with the resources he had and he sympathized with Charles' frustration. But for Charles, it wasn't enough. The man that killed his father remained free and something must be done, even if Charles was the one that had to do it.

As Charles entered the sheriff's office on this most recent visit to Martinez, he observed Hunsacker pacing anxiously behind his desk. He never knew the sheriff to be a nervous man, in fact quite the opposite. Hunsacker was about as calm and unemotional as they came, so this activity appeared out of character.

"Ah, you're here," Hunsacker said, finally noticing Charles in the doorway. "Please have a seat. Would you like a drink?"

Charles declined.

"I know you have other business in town, so I'll try to make this brief," Hunsacker continued. "I have been directed to cease the active pursuit of your father's killer at this time."

Charles heard the words clearly, but responded, "What did you say?"

"We can no longer spare the men or resources searching for someone who is long gone. Right now, I have deputies scattered all over the county looking for Moreno; one of them is more than a week's ride from here. This area is growing quickly and we need our lawmen to fulfill their required duties here in town. We simply cannot spare them anymore. I'm sorry."

Charles felt the frustration rising to a boil, and while it was not in his nature to yell out in anger, he could no longer contain himself. "That is unacceptable. My father's murderer remains free while you and your men will sit here and do nothing."

"Mr. Marsh, you know we have done everything we can to find this man." Hunsacker responded loudly, not willing to accept a label of complacency.

"It's not enough!" Charles shouted as he slammed his hand on the sheriff's desk. He got up from the chair and walked heatedly toward the door. "It appears," Charles continued, as he grabbed his hat off the rack and shoved it on his head, "that I will need to find this man myself."

Charles turned and flung the door open.

"Wait." Hunsacker said forcefully. "There is one thing I can offer."

Charles swung back around, not anticipating anything of much importance to be said. "What is it?"

"If you *are* going to try bringing this Moreno fellow to justice, it would be helpful for you … to be deputized."

This certainly was not what Charles expected to hear. In a much calmer tone brought on by the surprising statement, he replied, "I beg your pardon?"

"Look, as a deputy, you'll have the authority to arrest Moreno should you find him. It may also help when questioning people. Can't pay you, of course, but I can give you a badge."

Charles considered the proposition for several minutes and tried to visualize what it really meant. As near as he could tell, he was in for what quite possibly was a long and exhausting search for a man who most likely was in a completely different country. However, he was resolute. He made a promise to himself when he gazed at his father's face at the undertakers. How could he give up now?

Charles shut the office door, walked back toward Hunsacker, and looked him in the eye, "I'll take it…"

CHARLES WAS UNSURE WHERE to begin. He spoke to Sebrian a couple of times since his first meeting. Sebrian insisted that he had no idea where his son-in-law was and though Charles did not fully trust him, he believed at least this much. He had been told by his vaqueros that Sebrian and some of his men were asking around for information on Moreno's location, so it seemed likely that he really did not know where Felipe's whereabouts.

Also interesting to Charles was that, according to his sources, even after all these months Sebrian continued to search for Moreno locally. Why did he think Moreno would still be in the area? Perhaps to reconnect with his wife? Or perhaps there was another reason.

Amidst all his uncertainty, the one thing Charles was sure of was that he was not going to find his father's killer by staying at the Great Stone House. As difficult a decision as it was, he had to begin making his way toward Mexico where Moreno likely fled. He had, after all, a sketch of the man from the wanted posters, as well as a hefty sum of reward money. Someone will have seen this man. He just had to begin asking.

It took two weeks to make the necessary arrangements. Whit would oversee the ranch operations and Charles hired a manager, a Mr. Altman located in Martinez, to arrange any business transactions that needed to occur while he was away. They would correspond as often as possible about such matters.

Charles most worried about little Alice. Mrs. Thomson agreed to move into the Stone House as Alice's permanent caregiver. She would also oversee the home's upkeep with the Indian's assistance. Apparently, they still felt a loyalty to the family of the man who helped them so much.

Charles felt deeply conflicted about leaving Alice, but he knew she would be well cared for. He would write often and Mrs. Thomson promised to have Alice write him anytime he found himself in one place long enough to receive a letter.

So with as many details worked out as he could think of, Charles set out on horseback with a second pack horse in tow. With no specific location in mind and no way of knowing how long he would be gone, Charles headed south, where Mexico bordered the fledgling state of California.

THE CITY THAT LAY BEFORE Charles was larger than most of the other towns, ranches, or even missions that he visited on his quest. Six months of riding and six months of searching led to six months of frustration. He, of course, knew about the city of Los Angeles in the southern part of California, but this was the first time he had visited.

He recalled that Los Angeles was where his father first arrived when he reached the far west and it was where his father first declared that he was a physician – a self-proclaimed title that he held until his untimely death.

Charles began, as he had many times before, with a trip to the local saloon. He had already stopped by as many of the ranches and farms on the outskirts as he could locate. It was now late afternoon; the time when he hoped the saloon would be busiest and he would have the best opportunity to interact with the most people. Moreno was not much of a cattle hand, so Charles figured he would need to try to find work somewhere and perhaps someone will have noticed him.

A group of men leaned against the bar drinking; several others were scattered at tables. In one corner, a card game was in session. Charles would talk to all of them eventually, but he always started with the bartender; the one man that saw or heard the most. He sat on a stool and ordered a gin – a paying customer he reasoned, was more likely to retain the bartender's attention.

"Excuse me," Charles said when the drink was delivered. "I'm looking for someone and wonder if you may have seen him."

The bartender was a pleasant looking man, elderly with thin gray hair and a jolly face. "Well, now, who might that be?"

Charles unfolded the wanted poster that he carried inside his inner coat pocket, "...this man."

"Now just hold on a minute." The bartender reached under the counter – for some reason it always made Charles nervous when they did this, as if he was being too nosey and the sight of a shotgun ought to be enough to scare him away. It never happened, but Charles could not help feeling anxious. He was wrong again as the bartender retrieved a pair of spectacles and gingerly placed them on his face.

"Hmm...can't say for sure, but it looks a lot like that fella, Nino."

If Charles had been an animal of sort, his ears would have pricked up at this response from the bartender. Did he just say he recognized the picture?

"Who is Nino? Do you know where he is?"

"Used to work down the street at the hotel. He'd come in here a couple times a week, so I seen him a lot. Sure looks like him, but nobody called him Moreno ... just Nino I ever heard.

And what's this? Dang. If I'd a known there was a reward, I woulda said somethin' a long time ago."

"When was the last time you saw him?"

"Oh, musta been about a month. Couldn't say if he left town or just stopped coming in here. You can ask over at the hotel, they oughta know more."

"Thank you. Thank you very much," Charles said as he threw back the rest of the gin.

He hurriedly mounted his horse and began a quick trot in the direction of the hotel. His mind was racing with possibilities. He knew it was still a long shot and he made a conscious effort to not get overly hopeful, but this was the first lead he had in six months of searching. If it panned out, his journey could soon be over and he could return to the Great Stone House, and to Alice.

The hotel was a short distance away. Many of the buildings in Los Angeles were Spanish in design, given that just a short time ago it was under the governorship of Mexico. The hotel was no exception, with its white plastered walls and terracotta tile roof.

Charles entered the front lobby and asked a desk clerk to speak to the manager, declining to state the reason but insisting it was urgent. He did not like flashing his deputy badge, but in certain situations such as this, it was necessary.

The manager was a tall, thin man named Turner. He beckoned Charles into his office and then offered a chair. "Now Mr. Marsh...it is Marsh, isn't it?"

"That's correct."

"What can I do for you?"

"I need to know if you have seen this man." Again, Charles unfolded the poster and placed it on the desk.

156

Turner examined it quickly and proclaimed, "Why yes, I have. He goes by the name Nino. He worked here for about a month doing odds and ends, mostly cleaning, scrubbing pots in the kitchen, that sort of thing. Good gracious. A one-thousand dollar reward? Whatever did he do?"

Charles took a deep breath, overcome with emotion that he had finally… finally gotten closer to finding Moreno. "He murdered my father."

"Oh dear," responded Turner with a sincere look of sympathy. "I am very sorry."

"When was the last time you saw him?"

"He left three, maybe four weeks ago."

"Do you have any idea where he was headed?"

"All he said was that he was going north. Seems that he had some…I believe he said… other business opportunities."

CHAPTER 19

HARRISON AND CELESTE ARRIVED at his home in one of the numerous subdivisions strewn throughout the city. This was the first time Celeste had actually been inside, and Harrison was thankful that he was generally a clean and organized person thereby avoiding the potential embarrassment of a surprise visit.

His home was modest, but well kept. A small downstairs bedroom was converted into a study, which is where he led Celeste. He turned on the computer and waited for it to warm up. Celeste scanned the room, taking notice of the tasteful décor, somewhat surprising, she thought, for a single man living alone. The study walls were covered with a variety of wildlife and landscape photographs.

"Beautiful photos," Celeste remarked.

"Thanks," replied Harrison. "A hobby."

"You took all of these?" responded Celeste, genuinely surprised.

Harrison did not look up from the computer. "Uh … yeah."

"Very impressive, Mr. Barrett. Who are the kids in the photo?" she asked gesturing toward a framed picture standing on the desk.

"Niece and nephew."

"Very cute. How old?"

"I think they're eight and six in that picture and that was about a year ago."

They never talked about his extended family, or hers for that matter. Harrison knew that her divorce was an extremely sensitive topic and chose to stay clear of any conversation about family.

"How many siblings do you have?" she continued.

"Two sisters, one older, one younger. How about you?"

"Just a younger sister."

They shared a glance that exchanged more meaning than the words just spoken. It was a little more intimate.

"OK, here we are," he said, as the image of the paper found in the Old Stone House appeared on the computer screen - a large, irregularly shaped triangle with words in a foreign language, maybe two foreign languages, written at the corners. "I suggest we begin by trying to translate the words, maybe that will give some insight into what this is supposed to be, 'cause if it's a map, it's not like any map I've ever seen."

"Sounds good. Let me write the words down, then you can open up the Internet and we'll try Googling them. Pick a corner, any corner."

"OK," replied Harrison. "How about the one at the top. It says *domus lapideus*. Now I could be wrong, but that doesn't sound like any of the Native American words we've translated before. What do you think Ms. Foreign Language Teacher?"

"I'm guessing Latin. Plug it in and see what you get."

"First word – *domus*. Alright, we got a bunch of businesses, the last name of some people, and…OK, we've got something on Wikipedia."

"Really? What does it say?"

"*Domus*–'In ancient Rome, the **domus** - plural *domūs*, genitive *domūs* or *domī* - was the type of house occupied by the

159

upper classes and some wealthy freedmen during the Republican and Imperial eras'. Basically, I'd say it's the name of a house for the wealthy in Rome. Is that Latin? They spoke Latin, right?"

"Yes, Barre, they spoke Latin in Rome. Try the next word."

"*Lapideus* – got the name of a bunch of people again and the name of some places. Nothing in Wikipedia but here…Wiktionary says it's Latin meaning 'stone or made of stone'. Are you kidding me? The first corner of this triangle says 'House for the wealthy made of stone'."

"Gee," Celeste said as sarcastically as she could manage, "I wonder what *that* might refer to?" She continued, "This is exciting. I'm getting goose bumps."

Harrison continued, "Let's do this corner way out here to the left. Two words, first word is *akataha*. Not sounding very Latin anymore."

"No, it sounds a lot like the Sioux that we saw before, though. What do you get?"

"Uh…names. Just looks like a bunch of people's names. And none from the 1800s. Let me try going directly to a Sioux translation website. Maybe we can find it there."

Harrison searched for the next several minutes, trying a few different sites, perusing for the word.

"Aha!" he exclaimed.

Celeste was leaning next to him trying to view the screen. His outburst startled her. She whacked him on the shoulder. "Do you mind?"

"Sorry. Got the word. *Akataha* is Sioux, or Lakota as they call it here, for 'top'."

"OK, I'll buy that. Now try the other word that was with it – *wakatanka*."

"Wakatanka. Wakatanka. I like that, it's fun to say. Wakatanka. Wakatanka," Harrison repeated again.

"Alright, already. I admit it's a great word, but how 'bout you find out what it means. I recommend you just stay on the Sioux language websites."

"Way ahead of you. Look, right here." Harrison pointed at the monitor. "Apparently it means 'Great Spirit'. Now that is very cool. No idea what 'top of Great Spirit' has to do with anything, but it's pretty neat, nonetheless."

"Let's finish with the last corner of the triangle and then try piecing it together. More Sioux-looking words – *iyatakuni sni mni.*"

Harrison again searched for some time with Celeste still leaning next to him.

"So what we ended up with is that *mni* means 'water' and *iyatakuni sni* means 'gradually disappearing'. What is gradually disappearing water?" Celeste questioned.

"Could be evaporation, but I couldn't tell you what that has to do with anything else we've translated here," Harrison replied. "We've got one more line to translate under that same corner with the gradually disappearing water. This one looks like it's in Latin again, though - *hic jacet sepultus aurum.*"

Celeste read each word and waited for Harrison to find a translation for it; *hic* – 'here', *jacet* – 'lies', *sepultus* – 'buried'...

"Stop!" shouted Harrison.

Again Celeste lurched from being startled. "Would you stop that?"

161

"Yeah, sorry. But I know what that last word means – *aurum*. If you look at the periodic table of the elements in chemistry, you'll find each element represented by a two-letter symbol."

"Yes. We all learned that in high school."

"Quite right, my dear, but *I* teach it," Harrison continued, feeling somewhat full of himself for being able to explain this without having to rely on the Internet. "Ever wonder why the two-letter symbol doesn't always match up with the name of the element? Why is sodium represented as 'Na'? Why is iron represented as 'Fe'?"

"I don't know, Mr. Barrett, but I'm sure you'll tell me soon enough."

"Because the symbols are derived from the original Latin names for elements. Sodium was called Natrium. Iron was called Ferrum."

"So what does this have to do *aurum*?"

"The two letter abbreviation for aurum is Au. Take a look…"

Harrison pulled up an image of the periodic table on the monitor and moved the curser to the symbol 'Au'.

"Gold. It means gold!" Celeste shouted. "Put together, that last line says *here lies buried gold*."

Shut up." Harrison exclaimed. Could this really be a map of buried treasure?"

Harrison and Celeste sat and stared at the computer screen. At the upper corner of the triangle – 'house made of stone'; then the corner far to the left and down a little – 'top of Great Spirit'; then the last corner back to the right, down slightly – 'gradually disappearing water / here lies buried gold'.

But how was this a map? There were no directions, no scale, no geography, nothing that marked a buried treasure except the words 'house made of stone' at one corner of a triangle.

"I wonder..." muttered Harrison.

"What's that?"

"Hang on a minute," Harrison replied. He began rummaging through a desk drawer in his study, then through a second drawer. "Ha! Found it."

He unfolded a map of the San Francisco Bay Area and flipped it over to the side that displayed the East Bay. Celeste joined him at the desk as he carefully examined the map.

"Where do we suppose the Old Stone House is if it were on this map?"

"Well," pointed Celeste, "here's Brentwood, this is Marsh Creek Rd., so the house would be about here, in this open space."

Harrison took a pen and made an 'X' at the location on the map. "Excellent. Now, I just wonder..." He moved quickly back to the computer. Celeste followed.

"What are you doing?" She could see the energy and focus in his actions, and so was content not to question him more until he was ready.

Harrison browsed the computer for the next ten minutes. "Interesting...," he said finally.

"Would you mind telling me what you are looking for?"

"I thought I had heard this before, but I wanted to be sure. Look here. You remember we read in the Brentwood Historical Museum about the Native Americans in this area in the 1800s, the Ohlone, Miwok, and Yokuts?"

"Yes."

"Well, they all have creation myths. Stories about how their people, or mankind in general, came to be. Years ago, during a summer program, I remember learning that many local tribes' creation myths centered around one common place. Usually this was the place where the animal spirits brought forth humans: the home of the 'Great Spirit'."

Celeste, who became impatient waiting for Harrison to find whatever it was he was looking for, was now engrossed in the explanation. "Keep going. I'm starting to get those goose bumps again."

"I'm right there with you this time." Harrison jumped out of his chair and raced back to the map spread out on the desk. "If I'm figuring this out right, the 'top of the Great Spirit'…is here."

Harrison's finger landed firmly on the map. Celeste, now also hunched over the map, read the label, "Mt. Diablo…"

"The highest peak of Mt. Diablo rises over 3,800 feet and is surrounded by much lower foothills, so it stands towering over the region and is visible from much of Northern California. On a clear day, it can be seen from the Sierra-Nevada mountain range over 100 miles away.

Mt. Diablo was such a visible landmark in those days that the Natives gave it great significance. Even today, it's the most prominent feature in the entire County."

"So suppose that corner of the triangle does refer to Mt. Diablo, how will that help us figure out what the third corner means?"

"Let's see …" Harrison rushed back to his computer and hit the 'print' tab. The two stood staring quietly at his printer for what seemed like an extraordinarily long time.

Celeste leaned next to Harrison and whispered, "Might be time to get a new printer."

Harrison glared at her.

Finally, the document finished printing. Harrison snatched it from the tray and dashed back to the map. "If we put the top corner of the triangle that says 'house made of stone' where the Marsh home is located, then line up the left corner of the triangle that says 'top of Great Spirit' where Mt. Diablo is … oh, crap."

"What's the matter?"

"It's too far. The triangle is at a larger scale than my map."

"Can you shrink the image on the computer?"

Harrison looked up at Celeste. "Good thinking, Ms. Scott."

"I have my moments."

Harrison hurried back to his computer and began manipulating the image on the screen. He printed several copies, each at a slightly different scale and handed them one at a time to Celeste, who laid them on top of the area map.

"Here, this one works." she exclaimed.

Harrison raced back to her. "Are you ready for this?" he asked, his voice thick with anticipation.

"Show me what you got."

Harrison carefully lined up the two points, the house and the mountain. The third corner of the triangle, the one that read 'gradually disappearing water – here lies buried gold', landed to the southwest of Mt. Diablo and to the south east of the Great Stone House. The two teachers, stared at the map, their eyes fixated on the point of contact between their paper and the regional map below.

Several moments passed until Celeste casually leaned next to Harrison and again whispered, "Sure would be nice if this paper were transparent."

Harrison looked at her, then quickly reached across the desk and grabbed a pen. He pierced the overlaying paper directly at the triangle's third corner and made a mark on the map underneath. He tossed the paper aside and Celeste bent down and squinted at the tiny writing.

"What does it say? What does it say?"

"It says," Celeste responded, "…Vasco Caves."

CHAPTER XX

CHARLES ANXIOUSLY OPENED the letter from Mrs. Thomson. He never stopped worrying about his half-sister, Alice. He wrote to her as often as he could, but was rarely in one place long enough for a letter to be returned.

He had, of course, been back to the Great Stone House several times during those years. Each time he was in awe at how much she had grown. He took joy in seeing that she remained the bubbly, inquisitive child that he met when he first arrived at the John Marsh home. Surely the loss of her mother, then suddenly of her father, took an emotional toll, but she did not show it - to him at least.

As he read the letter, he suddenly stopped and closed his eyes. "How long has it been? How old is she now? Three years? Could I really have been gone for three years? That would make Alice...seven, now."

He was in San Diego, just north of the Mexican border. He had been there for nearly eight months, using the location as base camp for ventures into Mexican territory while looking for Felipe Moreno.

This letter, though, was from Mrs. Thomson, not from Alice as were most of the others. This alone was reason for apprehension. Was Alice sick? Did she get hurt? Or worse...?

The letter began by explaining that everyone was doing fine, which greatly relieved Charles, enabling him to breathe through the rest. The letter described how much Alice was growing and shared her activities. She still loved to visit the Indian village and play with the Indian children, though, Mrs. Thompson noted, the number of local Indians was in steady decline. Also discussed was how much Alice continued to learn.

"She is such a bright, young girl," Mrs. Thomson repeated often. And that is why she was writing.

The responsibilities of managing the upkeep of the Great Stone House were taking their toll on Mrs. Thomson and Alice needed more tutoring than she could provide. She needed proper schooling in science, arts, languages, and culture.

Moreover, she needed to be in a place with children other than just the Indians. Therefore, she and Alice would be leaving the Great Stone House and moving to Oakland, where they would live with relatives while Alice attended a girl's school.

This news hit Charles hard, but upon reflection, he knew it was inevitable. Alice would never be able to spend the rest of her life in the relative isolation of Rancho Los Meganos. He knew moving was in her best interest and was thankful for Mrs. Thomson's good judgment.

Still, it was difficult to accept that no one would live in his father's remarkable creation. John Marsh built the stone house for his wife, Abby, who died before ever stepping foot inside.

Then, just a few short months after moving in, Marsh's own life was taken. And now Alice, too, would abandon the home. Perhaps it was for the best. The house was too associated with tragedy. Perhaps it was never meant to be lived in.

Charles began making arrangements to start traveling again. His treks into Mexico were fruitless. No sign of Moreno and no leads on where to try next. Charles decided to head back to the Marsh house and assist with Mrs. Thomson and Alice's

168

move to Oakland. He also needed to check on the ranch's business affairs after learning that things were not going as well as he hoped.

CHARLES SAT IN THE STUDY and wrote notes about his inspection of the exterior of the Great Stone House. Several wall stones were dislodged and needed to be remortared. The railing of the second story balcony on the home's north side was loose and required repair. There were a number of leaks in the roof that also needed tending. To Charles, the house felt a bit like he did; tired, a little worn, and now … alone.

Alice and Mrs. Thomson moved out two days ago, just a week after he returned from San Diego. He helped load their wagon and buggy with Alice's belongings, along with some items belonging to their father. They all agreed to store as much as possible at Alice's new home to help make the transition as smooth as possible.

It was not just Alice that could not live in the house her father built. Charles too, realized the Great Stone House was just an empty shell now. The heart of the home, John Marsh, was gone. And now its warmth, his sister Alice, was also gone.

There was also that ache in his gut. The one that kept gnawing at him, continuously aggravating any possibility of contentment – he still had not found his father's murderer. The quest felt like the only thing still connecting Charles to his father, and he would not let it go - at least not yet.

Charles asked Whit to come by the house that morning to discuss ranch affairs. When he arrived, the two men settled in the study and the Indian woman brought in a serving tray of coffee.

Whit sipped from his cup and Charles could not help but notice how awkward he appeared using the china dishware. He was definitely more of the metal-mug-over-an-open-campfire kind of man. Charles imagined that even being indoors in the fancy house probably made him uncomfortable.

"Good to have you back, Mr. Marsh"

"Thanks, Whit. It's good to be back. I understand that we lost some more cattle last month."

"Yup. Broken fence on the north side. Eighty head either wondered out or, more likely, someone came and got 'em."

"You think it's the same rustlers that took them the last two times?"

"Hard to say, but I'd wager so. No trace of them, though, or the cows."

"Every cow was branded. Why can't they be found?"

"Well, if they was taken by a big enough operation, they'd just butcher 'em right away. Can't trace a brand on a slab 'a beef."

"Damn frustrating. How much was the loss?"

"You'd need to talk to Altman about that. I just try to keep the ranch running. That Altman fella you hired is the one that keeps track of the money."

Charles and Whit talked for another hour about conditions on the ranch. The conversation was distressing at best. Whit could manage the care and management of the cattle and horses, but he couldn't make decisions about when it was time to sell, how many, or for how much.

New breeding stock were needed, but from where, by whom, and at what cost? Equipment needed replacing or repair so someone needed to negotiate prices. Livestock feed costs were increasing – should they keep paying the higher prices or search for a new supplier? With no one actually running the ranch, these decisions were neglected.

In addition, with Dr. Marsh long gone, the Miwok that lived nearby and tended to the wheat fields and orchards left, partly on their own and partly due to harsh treatment by the vaqueros and other ranch hands.

Without the profits from selling the food crops, Charles reasoned, the financial balance was surely in the red. He knew it could not be sustained but was unsure what to do about it. He needed some advice from Mr. Altman.

THE TRAIL TO MR. ALTMAN'S PLACE in Martinez was the same trail that his father took three years ago when he was robbed and killed by three vaqueros. One of them, though, Moreno, was after something else - papers that he knew John Marsh was carrying – and he committed murder for them.

Charles still did not know what the papers were. He was certain they were related to the important journal that his father left for him, but was never able to make a connection. That journal was now in Alice's possession, stored somewhere at her new Oakland residence.

Charles' horse rounded a bend and entered a grove of familiar oak trees. Even after so many years, he knew this was where his father's death occurred. Sheriff Hunsacker took him there and showed him the exact spot where John Marsh's body was found.

His horse trotted as Charles tried to make good time to Martinez, but now he slowed his pace considerably and fixated on the rhythmic sound of horse hooves pounding the gravel trail.

He felt nauseous imagining the scene of his father's bloody corpse lying in a ditch on the side of the path. The oath that he made to himself to capture the man responsible weighed heavily on his heart. For three years he failed.

Moreno, or 'Nino' as he was apparently called, was still in California. He had to be. There were occasional leads; someone who recognized the now faded wanted posters, most often in or around Northern California, but Charles was never able to catch up with the evasive Moreno.

Still, he knew there was a reason Moreno remained in the area. That paper Moreno took from his father was linked to this region, and if this man was willing to kill for it, he wasn't likely to just abandon what he was searching for.

But that wasn't the only reason Charles felt sickened. He was on his way to meet with Mr. Altman – a meeting he very much dreaded. With the ranch finances doing so poorly, he feared there was going to be only one solution presented by Mr. Altman - and thinking about it broke Charles' heart.

The John Marsh Stone House[10]

CHAPTER 21

*V*ASCO CAVES REGIONAL PRESERVE *is home to a stunning and unique combination of resources. Spectacular rock outcrops break suddenly from the rolling eastern foothills of Mount Diablo, providing magnificent scenery for hikers and geologists alike. Though ancient, the Preserve's resources are extraordinarily fragile, and exist today because of the land's isolation and past efforts to keep it secret.*[11]

The words that appeared on the monitor transfixed Harrison and Celeste. The Google search results indicated that the area was owned and operated by the East Bay Regional Park District. The last line of the introduction on its webpage – 'isolation and past efforts to keep it a secret', was particularly intriguing. *If* John Marsh was going to hide gold without a trace for over 150 years, this was as likely a location as any.

Celeste turned to Harrison, "I think there's a visit to some caves in our future."

"I agree. But according to this website, you can only visit the site as part of a guided tour."

"When is the next one?"

"Let's see, this is May, so there's a tour next Saturday. Ms. Scott, would you be available to join me on a hiking excursion next Saturday morning?"

"Why, Mr. Barrett, I'd love to."

"Then it's a date." Harrison could not help but smile to himself. Celeste used the date reference at least twice before regarding their outings. He knew she was teasing him, so it felt good to tease her back.

THE WEEK AT WORK was a difficult one for both Harrison and Celeste. Maintaining focus on their classes was challenging given the anticipation of their visit to the caves the following weekend. In addition, Spring fever was in full epidemic proportions on campus, and they both found it nearly impossible to accomplish anything.

Every high school teacher knows the symptoms of and subsequent consequences for an infectious bout of Spring fever. First, the warmer the weather - the fewer the clothes. This was a chance for showing off fresh tans, newly pierced belly buttons, or as much leg as possible.

There was a school dress code, of course, but teenage girls are adept at tugging, straightening, stretching and generally managing to adjust their clothes to give the appearance that they actually fit prior to entering a classroom or walking past an administrator who might make them change.

Then, when out of sight of adults but in plain view of hormone-ridden, ogling teenage boys, the shorts shrank, stomachs appeared, and cleavage magically resurfaced. High school boys were already practically brain-dead with thoughts of the approaching summer break clogging their minds; mix in the distraction of girls adorned in spring plumage and most boys would be more productive sleeping on the sofa at home.

Second, were the specific conditions afflicting twelfth-graders. Both Harrison and Celeste had a number of students battling senioritis. For some, the disorder was brought on by acceptance to college, with no real need to earn good grades during the final quarter of the school year.

For others, it was caused by the knowledge that they were *not* going to college right after high school, and so, there was no real need to earn good grades during the final quarter of the school year.

Most teachers faced the challenge of battling Spring fever head-on; projects were due, essays were assigned, tests were particularly difficult. Typically, Harrison and Celeste would do the same, but for the past week at least, their preoccupation with the John Marsh mystery gave their students what amounted to a free pass.

Harrison picked Celeste up at her home that Saturday morning and they exchanged anecdotes from the prior week at school. The morning was already warm as they pulled into the staging area for the trip into Vasco Caves Regional Preserve. With a clear sky and no breeze, they knew temperatures would soar later that afternoon and both were glad this was an early morning excursion.

Various visitors gathered in the parking lot waiting for whomever would be their guide to give some initial directions. Then, just before the scheduled start time of 9 a.m., a light green truck from the Park District pulled in and out stepped the uniform clad naturalist that would show them the caves. He introduced himself as Richard Dix, but he told the 'folks' - as he referred to those joining him - to call him Rick.

"Ah…" Harrison whispered to Celeste, "Ranger Rick…"

Rick's lanky 6'4" frame was easy to follow as the group boarded a bus that would take them nearer the caves where they would begin the hiking portion of the tour.

Harrison and Celeste enjoyed their guide's boyish enthusiasm as he described some of the natural and cultural history of the area. Using language peppered with folksy jargon, they imagined that he would be equally entertaining to the adults that were on this trip as to the young school-age children that probably made up most of his clientele.

The trek began as a gradual ascent into the foothills. There were at least thirty other 'folks' in tow. Several older retired couples, a few families, some young couples, and one or two individuals, hailing from all over the Bay Area, came together to view this remarkably unique geologic formation - or so it was advertised.

Harrison and Celeste tried to stay close to Rick as they walked, soaking in every description in hopes that some tidbit might trigger a connection to the map they found in the Old Stone House or to any other fragment of information they had collected.

They hiked for a few miles delighting in the scenery – open grasslands spotted with large oaks and interlaced with an occasional tree-lined creek that provided a welcome oasis of shade. Rick paused regularly, both to allow stragglers to catch up and to point out a natural wonder or two, such as a soaring Golden Eagle or an endangered Red-legged Frog. Harrison, being the science geek that he was, was eating it up, and even Celeste thoroughly enjoyed herself.

"And there," Rick exclaimed after another few hundred yards, "is what we've come to see." He stood gazing in the direction of large rocky outcrops that looked as though the skin of an enormous animal had been scrapped away, exposing the bare bones beneath. As Rick explained, it was soil, however, not

177

skin, that had been eroded away by wind and water, revealing the harder sandstone below.

Permeating the sandstone were numerous caves of diverse shapes and sizes. They were not caves created by the typical water-dripping-through-limestone with which many people are familiar, with their stalagmites and hanging stalactites. Rather these caves were formed by winds sweeping through and carving out deep impressions into the sides of the formations. Rick continued his fascinating description of the area and again emphasized its uniqueness as the group proceeded toward the nearest outcrop.

"But here," he said with an enthusiastic smile, "is one of the coolest things about some of these caves." He crouched close to the rear wall of one chamber after directing the group to remain outside the opening. With a small flashlight, he highlighted a drawing, faint but visible, in rust colored pigment.

"The Native American pictographs are estimated to be anywhere from a few hundred to a few thousand years old. And it's only because of the Vasco Cave's isolation that they still exist. Harrison and Celeste leaned in as close as they could to get the best view of the pictograph and simultaneously uttered, "Oh my God…"

An elderly couple nearby gave them an odd look to which they were both oblivious. Harrison and Celeste looked at each other for a moment, then Harrison took Celeste by the arm and led her to the back of the group.

"Are you seeing what I'm seeing?" he questioned

"If you're seeing an ancient pictograph of a bird that looks exactly like the drawing that was stolen from Alex Moreno's home…then yes, I'm seeing what you're seeing."

"Yup, that's what I'm seeing. This is incredible. Alex's drawing has to be connected to this place. Perhaps the directions written below the drawing use the pictograph as a marker or starting point."

Both teachers felt the rush of adrenaline pulsing through them as they came to the same conclusion. If there was really buried gold, it might be somewhere nearby.

Harrison broke his gaze with Celeste, "I wonder, though...?" He worked his way back through the crowd to the front and raised his hand.

"Yes, sir?" Rick responded.

"Is this the only cave drawing in the area?"

"Not at all. There are dozens scattered throughout the hills for miles. This is just the easiest for us to view. We won't be able to get to most of the others."

"Then can you tell me, are there any other bird drawings that look like this one?"

"Yes, actually quite a few more. This bird symbol is the most common drawing we find."

"Oh, great..." Harrison responded sarcastically.

Rick cocked his head at Harrison, confused about the tone of his response. Harrison ignored him and walked back to join Celeste.

"Well, it's not going to be quite so straight forward."

"I guess not," she replied. "Then again, you didn't think a pot of gold was just going to fall into your lap, did you?" Celeste gave him a quick smile and began following their guide as he headed to the next stop.

Harrison caught up with her and continued thinking aloud. "There has to be more to the clues to help narrow it down. Apparently, these pictographs are spread out for miles."

The two teachers continued chatting for a while as the tour proceeded. The sun was rising higher and the air was warming. Rick pointed out a large gopher snake that was sunning itself in the middle of the path and discussed the Park District's work to restore some of the native plant life to the region.

He did a particularly long presentation about structures called 'concretions'. These noticeably surrounded most of the caves as almost perfectly spherical shaped stones protruding from the surrounding surface, most the size a beach ball or larger.

Rick explained the process of their formation as being slowly accreting layers of minerals deposited around a nucleus of some sort, usually a shell or other fossil, when the region was under water millions of years ago.

The round objects appeared unusual, even out of place in the free-formed environment of the hillsides, almost as if they had been thrown there by some prehistoric giants playing a game of catch. Normally Harrison would be fascinated, but for now he was lost in contemplation about other matters.

The group reached another expanse of rocky outcrops and Rick paused. "Ok, folks, gather 'round. This place you're standing in is home to one of the rarest geological features you'll find anywhere. It's the only place in the Preserve where you can find vernal pools."

Harrison heard the words and another dose of adrenalin shot through him. He clutched Celeste's arm and whispered to her. "Listen to this closely."

Rick continued with his description about pools of water that only existed during the spring, after winter rains and runoff formed small ponds. These ponds only lasted until summer when the sun's heat would evaporate them entirely. But during this brief time, extremely endangered critters would literally 'spring' to life to quickly feed and reproduce in the water before going dormant again.

The group huddled around several of the vernal pools to observe the Fairy Shrimp and Tiger Salamanders that Rick pointed out.

Celeste was again enthralled by the information, but turned to Harrison. "I don't get it. What's the connection?"

"This, my dear Ms. Scott, is the place of ... *gradually disappearing water.*"

Celeste felt a rush as goose bumps quickly covered her arms. "Oh my..."

But before she could finish her thought, Harrison turned away, once again making his way toward their guide.

"So, Rick, I was wondering... are there any of those bird pictographs near this area?"

"Yes, as a matter of fact. I believe that five or six have been documented in the caves just in this small valley. We won't be able to view any of them today, but they're similar to the one you saw earlier.

"Cool." Harrison replied. He shot a wink back to Celeste.

After taking some time to observe the Vernal Pools, Rick announced to the group that they would be heading back now, but he had one last bit of history to share with them first.

"This area," he proclaimed, "was once a hide-out for the infamous Joaquin Murrieta in the 1850s."

Celeste and Harrison's ears perked up, "What...
1850s...?" they both thought.

"Depending on whose story you believe, Murrieta was
either a ruthless bandit raiding and robbing ranchers and farmers
for profit, or was, as some have called him, the Mexican Robin
Hood. Some historians indicate that he had been brutally beaten
and his wife raped by Anglo-Americans who were jealous of his
success in the gold mines. This drove him to declare war on the
Anglos in California that 'stole' the land from Mexico."

One of the old timers in the crowd chimed in. "Wasn't
that how the legend of Zorro got started?"

"That's right. Joaquin Murrieta was the primary
inspiration for the fictional character, Zorro, who battled the evil
Anglo aggressors that stole his land and brutalized his family. Of
course, when Hollywood got a hold of Zorro, he tended to fight
evil Mexican overlords rather than white folk."

Harrison immediately turned to Celeste. "So let me get
this straight, it's possible we've determined the meaning of Alex's
drawing, we might know the location of the gradually
disappearing water, and now Zorro may be involved?"

"I know," Celeste whispered back, "this is getting
stranger by the minute."

She asked Rick a question. "Can you tell me what
happened to Joaquin Murrieta?"

"I'm glad you asked." Rick pulled out a copy of what
looked like an old poster. "In 1853, the California governor put a
price on his head and he was killed by some hired guns. To prove
they got their man, they chopped off his head, put it in a jar of
alcohol and displayed it around the State, charging one dollar to
view it."

A few gasps could be heard and one "cool" from a pre-teen boy in the group as Rick held up the poster with a sketch depicting Murrieta's head in a jar and advertising the tour.

"And the moral, ladies and gents," Rick continued, "... is that crime is not a way to get 'a-head' is this world."

A few groans were registered by the group as Celeste smirked at Harrison, "Oh, great, another punster. You two have a lot in common."

"Well," Celeste said to Harrison as the group commenced the hike back to the bus, "Ranger Rick said he died in 1853, but John Marsh was killed in 1856, so Murrieta couldn't have had anything to do with that murder."

"Yeah, I guess you're right."

"So what's the matter," Celeste said, observing the still confounded expression on Harrison's face.

He stopped, looked at her exasperated and responded, "Zorro...haven't we dealt with enough already? I can't believe that now ... it's Zorro!"

Celeste smiled. They turned to catch up with the rest of the 'folks'.

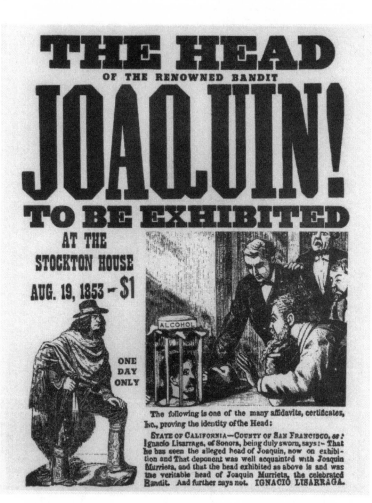

The Head of Joaquin Murrieta[11]

CHAPTER XXII

October 2, 1866

CHARLES SAT AT THE BAR, fumbling with his deputy star. He didn't wear it anymore. It was kept in a vest pocket. He was not even sure why, but he had been carrying it for ten years, so it seemed as much a part of getting dressed as putting on boots.

As he surveyed the scene in the saloon, he noted the usual characteristics: the permeating smell of alcohol, usually whiskey, mingling with the oaky wooden floors, the sound of men talking low and deep and often in rhythm with the lively tunes from a piano, and the familiar feel of a smooth glass in the hand.

He had visited this saloon in Sacramento before, maybe three or four years ago. It was one of hundreds, maybe even a thousand stops he had made over the past decade, so the details were indistinct. The bartender asked if he wanted a refill and Charles declined. "No, thank you. I need to get going. I'm looking for someone over at the hotel."

Charles recalled the conversation two weeks ago with the man who managed the Occidental Hotel in San Francisco. Someone who called himself 'Nino' and was similar in description to the sketch that Charles showed had worked at the hotel for two months. The last day on the job, he collected his pay and said that he was moving to Sacramento because of a better opportunity at the Willard Hotel.

That was where Charles was heading. He knew it was a tenuous lead, at best. After years of following such leads, rumors, hunches, and any manner of suspicion, the hope of one of them actually paying off deteriorated long ago. But he needed to try. After all, what else was he to do? He had spent his share of his father's fortune years ago.

Each time he made it back to Martinez, the meetings with Mr. Altman resulted in the selling of another portion of Rancho Los Meganos. Now, ten years later, the ranch was so whittled away that it was unrecognizable as the dominion his father once reigned over. Charles still owned a large portion of the land, the portion where the Great Stone House stood, but it could not last...he knew it would not last.

Even the house itself conveyed distress. The last time Charles stopped by the Great Stone House was six months ago. It tore at his soul to see it in such disrepair. With no one managing the maintenance it looked, he thought, as weary as he felt. Crumbled stones, broken shingles, weathered and worn porch boards and railings; even broken and boarded up windows all gave Charles the sense that he was losing his connection with the Great Stone House ...and with the memory of his father.

The hotel was situated near the railroad. As Charles sauntered through the dusty street, he could not help but contemplate the remarkable feat undertaken to link those tracks across the entire continental United States. The newspaper said completion was still a few years away, but just the attempt was remarkable, Charles thought. The project was started by a man whom his father knew and admired, Abraham Lincoln. Charles recalled reading notes in his father's journal about the respect he had for Mr. Lincoln. Had he been alive, he would have been pleased to witness Mr. Lincoln's ascension to the presidency.

Charles let his mind drift through memories of other events imbedded in the past ten years searching for his father's killer: a civil war came and went, President Lincoln was assassinated, and many of the small frontier towns that he traveled through had grown into full-fledged cities. Then there was Alice –dear, little Alice was already a young woman. How could so many years have passed?

Charles entered the hotel and asked to speak with the manager as he had done many times before. A short wait later, a thin, well-dressed man who looked to be in his twenties met Charles and introduced himself as the assistant manager.

"How may I be of service?" he asked.

"I'm looking for someone and was told he may be working here. His name is Felipe Moreno."

"And may I inquire as to why you are looking for him?"

Charles reached into his vest pocket and removed the deputy badge. "Just need to ask him some questions."

"Well, I'm afraid there is no one working here by that name. Do you know what he looks like?"

Charles reached into a vest pocket and pulled out a paper that he unfolded. The sketch of Moreno had been redrawn several times during the course of ten years. Sometimes because the previous papers were too worn or faded to use, sometimes because of a possible change in Moreno's features, such as shorter hair or addition of a mustache. This drawing was very similar to the original.

The assistant manager inspected the image closely. "I know a man that looks like this, but his name is not Felipe. He goes by Nino."

Charles' pulse immediately quickened and a large lump spontaneously formed in his throat. He inhaled deeply. "Don't get ahead of yourself," he thought.

"This man, Nino, does he still work here?"

"Yes. He was hired to assist in the kitchen, perhaps two weeks ago."

"May I speak with him?"

"Of course. I will get him. Please, have a seat."

Charles scanned the lobby. Patrons were coming and going as clerks assisted with luggage. A young, wealthy looking couple relaxed nearby, probably awaiting a carriage. Charles took a seat in one of the high-back chairs in the reception area of the hotel. He could feel the adrenaline pulsating through his veins. Was he ready for this? What if it really was Moreno? How would he know for sure? What would he say?

He had run through the scenarios in his head countless times over the years. There were even the instances when he met up with men who could have been Moreno, but turned out not to be. Could this be different? Why would it be?

The assistant manager retuned to the lobby followed by a short, dark-skinned Mexican. His age looked about right, thought Charles. About the right height. But still, how to be sure?

"This is Nino," the assistant manager said, gesturing to the man. Then added, "and this is...I'm sorry, I never got your name."

"Charles. Thank you. That will be all," he continued quickly, not wanting to be referred to as a deputy, nor as a Marsh.

"Please, have a seat," Charles said to Nino.

Nino, looking confused as to why he was there, took a chair directly across from Charles. The features, Charles again thought, are so similar, a bit rounder, older perhaps, but definitely like the sketch. Moreno had never seen him as far as he knew, so he was not worried about being identified. In addition, it had been ten years since his father's murder, so it was possible that Moreno had stopped worrying about being caught.

Charles leaned forward. "I was hired to deliver something to a man. Something very valuable. But I need to be sure that you are the man I'm looking for." Charles saw the reaction he was hoping for as Nino sat up a bit straighter and appeared to listen more intently.

"Are you Felipe Moreno?"

Nino's consideration of how to answer this question was obvious during the long pause.

"Si...yes. I am Felipe Moreno. What have you got for me?"

The anticipation was swelling in Charles and he forcefully released his grip on the arm of the chair in an attempt to calm himself before proceeding. Anyone could say he was Felipe Moreno, especially if he thought he was going to get something valuable. How could this man prove it?

"The item I am supposed to deliver was given to me by a relative of the man I am looking for, specifically, his father-in-law. Could you tell me who that might be?"

Again there was a delay as the man pondered the potential consequences of his response. Apparently, the possibility of obtaining an item of worth outweighed any negative consequences so the man answered. "I have not seen him for some time, but my father-in-law is named Sebrian, Ygnacio Sebrian."

It's him. The realization penetrated Charles as if he had just been shot in the chest. Him! With his body flooded by ten years of emotions, he was literally frozen. Frustration, anger, disappointment, all surged through his veins in one final wave of disbelief that his search was over – finally over.

Ten minutes ago, Charles felt nothing toward the man that sat across from him, but now, this was no longer just a man. This was Felipe Moreno, the man that murdered John Marsh. His hatred boiled to the surface. He had a gun, a small handgun that he wore inside his coat. It would be so easy to end this miserable journey, to repay the cost to his life – both emotionally and materially and to avenge his father's death right here…right now.

Charles slowly stood up. "Please excuse me for a moment."

He hoped that Moreno would assume that he was about to retrieve the item of their discussion. Charles met the assistant manager at the reception desk and whispered, "Get the sheriff here… now."

The assistant manager looked at Charles, and then glanced over at Moreno who was watching them. As he looked back into Charles eyes, the severity of the expression made it evident that he had better do as he was told and so he quickly retreated to the rear and out of sight.

As Charles turned around, Moreno was out of his chair and making his way toward the door, his suspicions apparently aroused. "No." thought Charles, "he will not get away."

The pistol felt warm and firm in his grip as he quickly pulled it from his jacket and pointed it at Moreno. "Do not move or I swear on my father's grave that I will shoot you in the back!"

The reception clerk and the young wealthy couple seated nearby all recoiled and ducked behind furniture and an elderly women guest screamed when she saw the gun.

Moreno stopped as directed. Motionless.

Charles replayed ten years of anguish in his mind. He cocked the pistol, now pointed directly at the back of Moreno's head. "Turn around."

Secretly, in a dark corner of his hardened heart, he hoped that Moreno would turn with a weapon in his hand, any weapon. The shooting, Charles reasoned, would be justified. There were plenty of witnesses that could give an account of the threatening actions requiring him to fire.

But it wasn't to be. Moreno turned slowly, his hands held out to his side, palms open.

The bewildered look on Moreno's face was almost comical. Who was this man and why was he pointing a gun?

Charles stood stationary for what, to him, seemed like an eternity, but was no more than a moment. And then... he eased the hammer on his pistol closed and lowered the aim of the weapon from Moreno's head to the middle of his chest. Charles took the deputy badge out of his pocket and with one hand pinned it onto the outside of his coat.

"Felipe Moreno, I am arresting you for the murder of Dr. John Marsh."

Another gasp was audible from the bystanders, as several more hotel guests stopped to witness the incident.

Still perplexed, Felipe cocked his head and squinted slightly, trying to bring the stranger into recognition. "Who are you?"

"My name is Charles Marsh. Ten years ago, you killed my father. And now, you bastard… justice will be done."

CHAPTER 23

66 ZORRO... I STILL CAN'T BELIEVE it's Zorro."

"You really need to let that go," Celeste said to Harrison with a grin. "Besides, it wasn't really Zorro. It was Joaquin Murrieta. Zorro wasn't even real."

"The whole thing is just so weird. Zorro was one of my heroes when I was a little kid. I even dressed up as him for Halloween when I was, like, five. And now, I'm somehow involved in a mystery where the *real* Zorro might be a participant. Weird ..."

Harrison and Celeste took in lunch at a downtown café after their morning excursion to Vasco Caves in the shadow of Mt. Diablo. As they debriefed, Celeste kept glancing over Harrison's shoulder.

"What is it? What do you keep looking at?"

"I think this whole thing is getting me paranoid. But it sure looks like that guy in the corner is watching us."

Harrison began to turn around. "Don't look, silly." she whispered loudly.

"Probably the parent of some kid you flunked."

"Definitely not a parent I've ever met. Looks way too mean."

"OK, since you won't let me turn around, describe him."

"Brown skin, black curly hair. Looks Hispanic from here. Oh, geez..."

"What?"

"He's getting up and leaving. I think he saw me staring at him. Hmm …interesting."

"What's that?"

"Walks with a limp."

Harrison instantly recounted in his mind events of the past few weeks. "Which leg is bad?"

"Um…looks like his left leg."

"Can you see his face?"

"Not any more. He walked outside. But it looks like he's going to walk right by the window. There… that's the guy."

As the man walked by the café window at a rapid pace, Harrison stared intensely at his face. The man gave a quick glance in their direction and then increased his speed to almost a jog, limping badly on one leg.

"His mouth. Did you see his mouth?"

"What about it?"

"He had an obvious fat lip. You could still see the cut."

Celeste finally caught on to Harrison's questioning. "Oh my gosh. That was the guy that attacked us in the Old Stone House."

"Yeah, I think so. Come on."

Harrison quickly left some money for the meal and they dashed out of the café. It was too late. The man had disappeared.

"Let's go, Barre. We need to get back to the police."

The police department was a short distance from the café. They spoke directly with the ranking officer on duty who noted the description of the man and immediately put out a bulletin to patrol officers in the area. He assured them that they would be notified if contact was made.

194

As they exited the police station, Celeste turned to Harrison, "Barre, I'm nervous. It seems clear that someone has been following one or both of us. He obviously knows what we're looking for."

"And," Harrison continued, "I'd wager he's the same one who broke into the home of Alex's family."

"You really think so?"

"Not only that, let me toss out something else to think about. We stumbled onto this whole buried gold thing by following the work that Alex was doing before he died. And it seems to connect directly back to the drawing that the Moreno's had hanging in their home – passed down through generations, remember?"

"Yes, I remember."

"I don't think Alex killed himself, C."

"I don't follow."

I think Alex may have been murdered."

"What?! Oh my God, Barre, are you serious?"

"Too many coincidences. Too many connections. Somehow, Alex got caught up in this buried gold mystery and I think it cost him his life."

"We need to tell the police. We need to tell his parents."

"Well, we've already given the police all the actual evidence we have. Everything else is just suspicions. But you're right; we definitely need to talk to his parents again."

THE DRIVE TO THE HOME of Alex's parents was short. The two teachers once again found themselves in the neighborhood of modest single story houses and large well-aged trees. Harrison remembered the house from their previous visit and parked directly in front.

"Hey, would you mind grabbing my notes off of the back seat?" he asked Celeste.

"Not a problem." She reached for the binder that contained all of the translations, diagrams, and general information that they had acquired. "Very organized, Mr. Barrett. I'm impressed."

"Staying organized is the only way I stay sane," he smiled.

After knocking on the door, they were greeted by the sound of a yapping dog. Harrison forgot about the Chihua-rat and was sincerely hoping that Gabrielle would be there to escort the dog away. Alex's mother answered the door and Gabrielle did appear from behind and grabbed the dog on cue. She immediately recognized the teachers and invited them in.

It was late afternoon. Mrs. Moreno had been preparing supper. The aroma of fresh tortillas and peppers permeated the home.

"We are so sorry to bother you again," Celeste began, "but there is something very important that we would like to discuss."

Alex's father was not home even though it was the weekend. He recently acquired work as a landscaper, so Harrison and Celeste sat with Mrs. Moreno in the living room. They proceeded to describe their discoveries. Harrison referred to items in his binder and Celeste did her best to translate into Spanish some of the terms that Mrs. Moreno had difficulty understanding, such as Indian pictographs and vernal pools.

They had not discussed exactly how they would tell Alex's mom of their suspicion about his death. As the story wound to a close, they looked at each other and both wished that they had.

Celeste put her hand on Mrs. Moreno's arm. "Given all of these details, Harrison ... Mr. Barrett ... and I believe there is a possibility that Alex... did not kill himself. That is...we think ... that he ... may have been murdered."

They waited anxiously for Mrs. Moreno's expression to change, but it did not. At first Celeste thought that she did not understand what was said so she began to repeat herself in Spanish but Mrs. Moreno quickly stopped her.

"Yes, I understand." She stood up and walked to the large family photo over the fireplace. "I never believed that Alex could have taken his own life. But everyone said that is what happened. I never thought so. He would never have done that." She turned back toward Harrison and Celeste. "Have you told the police?"

"Well," Harrison responded, "they know everything we know, they just haven't put all the pieces together, yet."

"Then please...please let me know if there is anything I can do to help find who killed him; who killed my precious son."

Harrison and Celeste looked at each other, aching with sympathy and wondering whether sharing their suspicion was really the right thing to do.

"We would like to know more about the picture that was stolen," said Harrison. "Is there anything you can tell us about where or how you got it?"

'Excuse me for a moment," Mrs. Moreno said. She then left the room.

Harrison gave Celeste an inquisitive glance. Celeste shrugged.

A few moments later, she returned with a large binder that looked like a scrapbook. "I used to be much better about keeping up with this," she said as she opened the book revealing a few color-faded photographs. It was easy to tell that they were of her and her husband when they were young, probably in their twenties. Mrs. Moreno's features where fuller now, but the same. She had aged very well. And although they had not personally met Alex's father, they could tell that the young man in the album was the same as the adult in the family portrait over the fireplace.

"Alex's father got the picture from his father. He wrote it all down on a piece of paper here." Mrs. Moreno spent a few minutes flipping through the album until finally stopping on a page that contained a paper with hand-written words – all in Spanish. She handed it to Celeste who began translating.

"It basically describes Alex's dad Alfredo's family tree. She confirmed this with Alex's mom. It listed Alfredo's siblings and also the name of Alex's grandfather and his grandfather's siblings, but not his grandmother.

"This is interesting," Celeste interjected. "Next to Alex's dad and next to his grandfather is a bird symbol that looks a lot like the bird drawing in the stolen picture."

"That *is* interesting," Harrison responded. "Maybe it indicates who in the family has, or had, the picture. Does it go back any farther?"

"Oh, yeah. Way back by the looks of it. Hang on and let me try to sort it out."

Celeste grabbed a blank paper from Harrison's binder and began jotting down some details – father, grandfather, great grandfather …

They sat quietly for nearly ten minutes as she worked on translating the information.

"Ok, here is what I've come up with. If that bird symbol does actually track who in the family was in possession of the picture, then it goes back to Alex's great, great, great, grandfather - I think I counted that right – who gave it to his son, Alfredo, who was born in 1862, who gave it to his son, Alejandro, born in 1890, etc., until Alex's dad, also named Alfredo, was given it."

Harrison responded, "Well, they definitely must have thought it was really important to have kept track of it so closely. So, I guess we really have two other questions - who had it to begin with and where did that person get it?"

"According to this, it began with a man born in 1837 named Felipe."

Harrison froze.

"Uh oh," said Celeste. "You've got one of those looks again. What is it?"

Harrison quickly grabbed the binder with his notes and frantically began sorting through pages.

"What? What is it?"

"Here," he said, nearly out of breath. "I think I just found the answer to both those questions."

It was a copy of an article they had found at the Historical Society describing the murder of John Marsh.

"It says here that Dr. John Marsh was murdered on his way to Martinez by three vaqueros. One was never caught, one was released because he turned state's evidence against the third, who was eventually caught and convicted. The name of that third man… was Felipe Moreno – Alex's great, great, great, grandfather."

"Oh, my gosh. Are you sure?"

"It has to be. The dates all fit perfectly. The article said it was a robbery, but I think that Felipe Moreno stole more than just money. I think he stole a map, or at least part of a map, that he knew led to Marsh's buried gold - but he must not have had the other parts. It must have been passed down through his family for generations; each one telling the next how valuable it would be one day."

"And maybe someone else knew about the map, and that's why it was stolen," Celeste added.

"And maybe why Alex was killed …" exclaimed Harrison.

"It's getting late, Barre. We have work tomorrow and we're interrupting their dinner. We better get going."

The two said good-bye to Alex's mom, reassuring her that they would do everything they could to get to the bottom of what really may have happened to Alex and that they would let her know if they found out anything new.

As they headed back to Harrison's car, he noticed the perplexed look on Celeste's face. "What is it?"

"If we're right about all of this, then a boy was killed for this mysterious buried gold. I just wonder how much money we're actually talking about. I mean, this was over a hundred-and-fifty years ago. How much could it have been?"

"Good question."

"I'll try doing a little research on it tonight and stop by your classroom after school tomorrow. Sound OK?"

"Sounds great. While you're researching that, I better figure out what the heck I'm doing in class tomorrow," he said with a grin that indicated to Celeste he was only partly kidding.

Harrison drove back to Celeste's home to drop her off after their full day's excursion. With his car idling in her driveway, he said teasingly, "Well I enjoyed our date."

Then something happened that both shocked and confused Harrison. Celeste leaned over, kissed him on the cheek, and responded, "See you tomorrow."

Without looking back she exited the car and disappeared into her house.

CHAPTER XXIV

April 14, 1867

THE TRIAL WAS RELATIVELY quick, for which Charles was thankful. The motive was clear and Jose Olivas' sworn statement naming Felipe Moreno as the killer was enough evidence for the jury to convict. The guilty verdict still echoed in Charles' ears as if it were the first sound he'd heard clearly in over ten years. It was much more than the announcement of a man being convicted of a crime; it was the declaration of his own freedom.

For more a decade, Charles confined himself to a self-made prison of determination to track down the man who murdered his father. And now that it was finally over, he was released from the burden he shouldered for so long. The release made him both joyous and anxious.

It was, after all, the relentless pursuit of Felipe Moreno that kept him connected to his father, if only indirectly. Now that this journey was over, Charles actually felt a sense of loss; a feeling that the faint memory of his father that he still possessed would fade and be gone forever.

The Martinez courtroom was filled to capacity with various onlookers, journalists, friends and business associates of John Marsh, all awaiting with great anticipation, as was Charles, the reading of the sentencing by the county judge presiding over the trial. Three days passed since the jury stated its findings and Charles could barely contain himself, eating little and rarely sleeping.

The sentence was the final piece needed to obtain closure for this phase of his life; to put to sleep the long, often dark obsession with which he was so entwined and to allow an awakening back into a life with some sort of normalcy and promise.

The sentence was read. While the rest of the courtroom was abuzz with reaction and commentary, Charles sat motionless and said nothing. There was really only one outcome that he felt... that he knew... was appropriate for the act committed by this man – an eye for an eye.

But that was not the case. Charles slowly realized that he would not be witness to his father's killer put to death. He would not see the ultimate end of this ordeal. The judge's sentence – prison for the rest of his natural life – was not what Charles expected.

As he sat calmly lost in his thoughts, Charles tried to reason with himself ... perhaps this is better. This man had taken his father's life and stolen so many years of his own, perhaps being forced to spend the rest of his days within the miserable bonds of a prison was a more fitting punishment. Each day, then, he would be forced to think about how his actions one late September day eleven years ago resulted in his now wretched and tragic situation.

"Yes," thought Charles, "a tormented existence for the rest of his life is what he deserved, rather than the quick, painless release at the end of the hangman's noose."

As Moreno was led away, hands and feet now shackled so that the clanking of the chains and shuffle of his steps provided a rhythmic cadence, Charles was overcome by one last desire; one last contact before eliminating this man from his conscience. One last question he needed answered.

THE PAPERS SCATTERED ABOUT the desk and the dusty shelves would have been clear indicators that Sheriff Hunsacker no longer worked out of the Martinez office had Charles not already known this. In fact, he had been gone for years and Charles had lost track of where.

He knew his request of the current sheriff was unusual; one last meeting with a convicted man before he was taken away forever. He hoped the sheriff would understand. As it turns out, his worries were unfounded. The sheriff had no problem allowing Charles to spend some time speaking with Moreno in one of the jail cells in which he was held until transport the following day.

The cell was small. Much smaller than Charles had anticipated, so when he sat in the chair placed inside by the sheriff, he found himself much closer to Moreno than felt comfortable. Moreno watched him, suspiciously, without saying a word. Charles pondered for some time how he would broach the topic and realized that there was nothing else he could do but be direct.

"When you killed my father, you took something from him. More than just money. You took a paper. It is what he was killed for. What was that paper?"

Moreno looked away. "Why should I talk to you?"

"The rest of your life will be spent in prison, wasted and worthless. Why *shouldn't* you talk to me?"

Moreno was silent.

"I know it had something to do with my father's gold. What was it and how did you know about it?"

Moreno, who appeared more depressed than defiant, sat in silent consideration. He then spoke. "Three years before I worked with your father, when I was young, maybe sixteen years old, I rode with a bandito. My parents died in Mexico and I had nothing. He took me in."

"Who was the bandit?"

"He was Joaquin Murrieta, the great Mexican savior."

"The ruthless thief and murderer, you mean..."

"So you say. He told me about the gold coins that Señor Marsh had buried somewhere on his property. If we could find it, we would be rich. When I married Ygnacio Sebrian's daughter, I left Murrieta. He was killed soon after that."

Charles listened, contemplating each word. "So how did you find out about the paper?"

"When I told Sebrian about the gold, he became obsessed with finding it. When he could not do it on his own, that is when he convinced your father to hire me. I could then watch him and listen. Sebrian also paid other men to inform him of what they heard. We knew there was gold. We knew there was a map."

"How did you know my father had the map the day he was killed?"

"I heard him talking. Sebrian said that his other man learned the map was spread onto at least three separate papers. When I heard Señor Marsh talk about going to San Francisco, he said he had important papers that needed to be stored safely there. I knew this was the map."

"But he didn't have the map with him ..."

Moreno looked up into Charles eyes. This was the first time since they began talking that he lifted his view from the floor. "He did not have *all* of the map."

"So you killed him."

"He would not give me the rest. He would not say where it was."

"And now, where is the portion of the map that you took?"

Moreno returned his gaze to the floor and gave a half-hearted chuckle. "I do not think you will need it. Unless you have the other pieces, you will not be able to find anything. I have tried for many years. I think... that I will save you that pain."

"Does Sebrian know where it is?"

With a glance up to Charles that was filled as much with disgust as any other emotion, Moreno responded. "If I had told him where it was, do you think I would be alive to tell you this story now?"

Charles was stunned. He never felt that he could completely trust Sebrian, but he did not sense that he was a killer. Perhaps, he now thought, Sebrian was not someone who could kill, but rather someone who could pay to have it done. And though he could not get Moreno to admit that Sebrian told him to murder his father, there was no doubt in Charles' mind ... that is what happened.

CHAPTER 25

IT WAS NEARLY 4 P.M. when Harrison arrived at Celeste's classroom. Most students, including the ones she helped after school, were gone for the day.

"Hey, C. How'd your day go?"

"Oh, Barre, you're here. Hurry, come on over and sit. I've got something to show you and it's been killing me trying to wait until after school."

Celeste grabbed a paper off of her desk and the two sat in adjacent student desks near the front of the room. "OK, so I did some research online last night trying to get an estimate of how much money we might be talking about, *if*, of course, there actually is any. Are you ready for this?"

"I think so."

"So, I'm going to give you a low end figure and a high end."

"Lay it on me."

"All of the articles indicate that John Marsh supposedly buried forty-thousand dollars' worth of gold on his property. It's not clear how anyone knows this, but the stories are consistent, so let's assume that it's accurate."

"OK, I'm with you."

"In the 1850s, gold was about twenty-one dollars an ounce, so forty-thousand divided by twenty-one gives us 1,904.76 ounces of gold dust or nuggets. Now, since I'm not the math whiz that you are, let's round it off to an even two-thousand ounces of gold.

"Alright. Sounds reasonable."

The current price of gold is at a record level, near eighteen-hundred dollars an ounce. So eighteen-hundred times two-thousand gives us three-million-six-hundred-thousand dollars' worth of gold!

"Geez. People have killed for a lot less than that. So what's the low end figure?"

"That *was* the low end"

"You're kidding?"

"Now several accounts indicated that the forty thousand dollars was actually made up of gold coins. It's likely that if they were gold coins they were the $20 Liberty 'No Motto' coins. These were the ones minted in San Francisco around that time, so it makes sense. After a little calculating, forty thousand dollars divided by twenty dollars per coin equals two thousand coins."

"Got it ... possible that two thousand gold coins were buried."

"Ah, yes," Celeste said, getting more animated as she spoke. "But here's the really interesting thing. A circa 1850 $20 Liberty 'No Motto' gold coin is no longer worth twenty dollars. They're rare, and collectors pay a lot more for them."

"Yeah? How much more?" Harrison questioned.

"Anywhere from two-thousand dollars to twenty-thousand dollars and up, depending on condition."

"Shut up..."

"I'm serious. Let's assume these are in great condition since they've been out of circulation. That gives us twenty-thousand dollars times two-thousand coins equals, oh, I don't know ... how does forty million dollars sound?"

"What the ...?!"

"Exactly," said Celeste. "Pretty clear now why someone would go to all this trouble – and maybe even kill."

"And do you realize how close we may be to finding it?"

"Maybe," Celeste responded hesitantly. "But it's getting way too dangerous. We have to leave it up to the police."

Harrison stared out the window with a look that made Celeste nervous. "...Perhaps," he said.

BY THE TIME HARRISON made it to the vernal pools at Vasco Caves, it was close to midnight. The moon was nearly full and bright enough for him to hike the entire way from his car without a flashlight. There was no sign of the caretaker and he felt confident he could search for a few hours without being caught and still get back home for some sleep before getting up for work the next day.

The usual fanny-pack he carried had given way to a full backpack on which he hung a pick and a shovel. "Just in case," Harrison thought to himself, "... just in case."

There were several cave formations visible from the site of the vernal pools. Harrison began his search for the bird symbol in the one closest. The symbol, he reasoned, that would indicate the starting point for walking off the appropriate steps as described in Gabrielle's copy of the Moreno's picture.

The night air was perfectly still and quiet, interrupted occasionally by a howling coyote that set an eerie tone for his exploration. The naturalist that led the previous hike discussed how the ancient Native Americans considered the area very sacred and spiritual, and now Harrison could fully understand why.

He scoured the first cave with no success. No bird symbol. No pictographs of any kind. He paused momentarily before heading toward the next formation, distracted by rustling leaves nearby - probably his imagination. Hopefully not those coyotes...

The second cave was larger than the first, though further from the vernal pools. Immediately, Harrison noticed the faint outlines of drawings on the cave walls. He quickly directed his flashlight ... some geometric shapes and other coloring that was too faded to make out. Then, a few feet to the left, he saw it. Faint but clearly recognizable ...the bird symbol. The same crossing cigar-shapes with defined beak and indications of feathers. He flung off his backpack and pulled out the picture. It was the same.

As calm and logical as he always tried to remain, Harrison couldn't help but allow himself to get excited, even vocalizing "yes!" to no one other than the coyotes.

Now, with a giddy enthusiasm, Harrison snatched up the shovel and backed up directly in front of the bird symbol. This particular cave was some twenty feet deep and forty feet wide. Out of his pocket, he took a compass and lined it up. "OK, here we go," he whispered to himself.

Thirteen Steps West. This direction took him directly parallel to the back wall of the cave. He counted off steps, concentrating intensely on being consistent with the length of each; imagining what a 'step' might have meant to a man 150 years ago.

Eight Steps South. He adjusted the compass, turned left, and began stepping. He was now near the cave opening.

Sixteen Steps West. Harrison made a right turn, then paced off the remaining steps and stood staring at the ground beneath his feet. He ended up at the outer corner of one side of the formation. It seemed, he thought, a strange place to bury a treasure; nothing particularly special about this piece of dirt. Still, maybe that was the point.

"Only one thing to do now," Harrison said aloud, this time intentionally directing the comment to any curious coyotes.

As he started to dig, he was thankful for deciding to bring along the pick. While the soil was not impenetrable, it was definitely easier to chop it up before scooping with a shovel. He retrieved the pick, then with great effort, Harrison swung away.

Just a few minutes passed, but Harrison felt he made good progress. What was unclear, however, was just how deep he was prepared to go; a foot, two feet, six, ten...? A few more swings, some more shoveling; then Harrison froze - he was sure he saw something move. It was in the shadow of the moonlight about thirty yards away behind a pile of boulders. The thought of being watched that closely by the coyotes made him very uneasy.

One good scare ought to send them on their way, he reasoned. With shovel in hand, he cautiously approached the stones.

"Just keep digging."

The voice so startled Harrison that he nearly screamed, somehow managing to contain it while instinctively raising the shovel in preparation to defend himself. The possibilities raced through his mind. Certainly not a coyote... but who was it? Not the caretaker; he wouldn't have said to keep digging. Someone must have followed him.

Harrison then realized ... it had to be the curly-haired man that attacked them at the Old Stone House. The voice had a similar Spanish accent. And while Harrison could not see the man, he'd bet anything that he walked with a limp – the same man that they saw at the café. This is not good, he reasoned; not good at all.

"Who are you?" Harrison shouted, hoping to disguise just how nervous he was.

A shadowy figure emerged from behind the boulders. The sound of an uneven gait on the gravel exposed the man's hobble even before he was visible. Harrison stood his ground as he approached. The moonlight reflected off an object in his outstretched hand revealing the weapon, presumably the same gun that was used in the stone house; the man must have retrieved it from the floor after Harrison and Celeste fled.

"You will keep digging."

"Who are you and why have you been following me?"

"You know why. Now dig!"

The click of the gun hammer was audible causing Harrison to instinctively flinch. "Alright, alright... I'm digging." He turned back toward the hole he had begun and resumed shoveling.

The curly-haired man walked closer but stopped at least ten feet away, possibly remembering their last encounter when Harrison was able to disarm him. Harrison also figured that this man would not again be so foolish as to allow him to get too near. For now, he needed to do exactly as he was told.

The hole was a foot deep and about four feet in diameter. Harrison stopped shoveling and reached to grab the pick. "Do not try anything like before or I *will* shoot you," the man said.

The statement confirmed that this really was the same person from the stone house and the realization gave Harrison another jolt of anxiety, knowing this man must have been following him for days. But how much did he know? And how did he know it? Somehow, Harrison had to get some answers.

The weather was cool, but not cold. A perfect night for digging, Harrison thought, if not for the fact that he had a gun pointed at him. "So, how long have you been following me?"

There was a delay in the response, and then the curly-haired man finally replied, "Since you went to the house of the boy."

Harrison felt that engaging the man in any form of conversation was important so he was glad to get an answer. But that initial optimism was immediately stifled when he thought more about it. This man knew about the Morenos and, more specifically, knew about Alex – 'that boy'. He had to be the one that broke in and stole the document from their wall, but could he also be involved in Alex's death? A death that, to Harrison at least, appeared less and less like a suicide. If so, this man was dangerous – very dangerous.

The hole was now over two feet deep. The cool night air couldn't prevent Harrison from sweating and he paused periodically to wipe his brow or to switch from shovel to pick. All the while, the curly-haired man remained in the distance; the outline of his body and silhouette of his gun clearly visible, but the details of his features, other than the now familiar curly hair, were too faint to make out.

Three feet deep. "There is nothing here. How far down do you expect me to go?" Harrison asked as the sweat continued to accumulate on his shirt.

"Just keep digging. I'll tell you when to stop."

"How did you know about the map?" asked Harrison.

"I've known about it for a long, long time. I just did not know where it was."

This answer was not what Harrison was expecting and it intrigued him. "How did you know the boy, Alex Moreno?"

Instantly, the tone of the curly-haired man's voice became severe, "Enough! Keep digging."

The hole was nearly five feet deep now, with no sign of anything unusual. "Look, there is nothing here. We can dig all night long and won't find anything. It must not be the right spot. Maybe I marked it off wrong."

There was another long pause as it appeared that the statement was being considered. "Alright. Try it again. Try marking it off again. And remember, no one will hear a gunshot way out here."

Harrison knew he was right about that, but he also knew that he needed to do something. What was going to happen if daylight came and nothing was found? Harrison didn't like the possibilities. He slowly pulled out the map directions, being sure the curly-haired man saw he wasn't reaching for anything suspicious, and walked back to the bird symbol painted on the cave wall. What could he do? How could he let someone know of his circumstance should things go bad?

"OK, I'm going to try walking this off again. Maybe my steps were not the right size or maybe I counted wrong."

"Be quick."

Harrison faced the wall and knelt down directly in front of the bird symbol, pretending to be studying the map directions. He was, however, squeezing moisture out of his sweat-drenched

214

shirt. He grabbed a handful of soil and quickly worked it into mud, then stood up and turned away from wall, keeping his right hand behind his back while still considering the directions. The tint of the mud, he reasoned, would be visible, but not so obvious that his captor would notice it in the dark.

Whatever it is that he chose to write had to be significant enough to announce his situation, but not be confused with the graffiti of some wayward teenager.

Just one word came to mind, so he spelled it out, carefully concentrating to form each letter backward so it would be legible for someone facing the wall.

ANOTHER TWO HOURS went by. More pacing. More digging. Same results. The sun was beginning to rise and Mt. Diablo took on an orange glow that Harrison would have truly appreciated had he not been so uncertain about his predicament. The brighter the sky became, the more uneasy he felt.

Finally, the man, whose features were now becoming more apparent in the dawn with his dark skin, curly black hair, and clearly broken lip said, "Enough digging. You will come with me."

Harrison was surprised and somewhat relieved. He would still have a gun pointed at him and be this man's hostage, but at least he'd remain alive … for now.

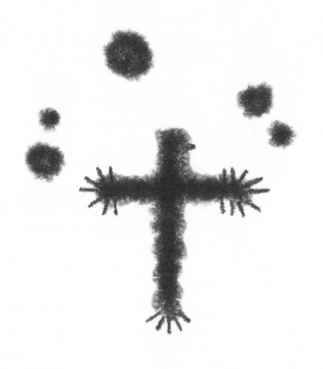

Bird Pictograph from Vasco Caves[12]

CHAPTER XXVI

May 23, 1867

SEBRIAN. THE MAN WITH WHOM John Marsh was in bitter conflict. The man who claimed knowledge about hidden gold. The man whose calm and cordial disposition made Charles' stomach churn. This was the man that Charles knew in his gut was responsible for arranging the murder of his father. His bitterness grew stronger with each passing thought.

Charles had worked so long and so hard to finally bring his father's killer to justice, but now there was a new objective: someone else who should pay a price. But what price? And how? The accusations of a condemned man would not be enough to convict for conspiracy to murder. How could he get evidence? Charles only knew one way to proceed; he had to confront Sebrian.

Much of the rangeland that Charles passed through on his way to the Sebrian ranch was no longer in his family's possession. The trail crossed fences of four different landowners from the original border of Rancho Los Meganos to the Great Stone House.

Thus far, Charles managed to keep a relatively small parcel that encompassed the house and allowed for some orchards and a small herd of cattle and horses. Unless his business ventures took a drastic change for the better, and soon, he was afraid that this property too would be a thing of the past – and it would break his heart.

But for now, he was once again focused on vengeance, or at least justice. He was no longer sure what his motives were for continuing the pursuit of someone that may or may not be involved with his father's death. He just knew he had to follow the trail as far as it would take him.

Charles' stop at the Great Stone House was brief. The cool fall days were beginning to give way to winter's chill and Charles wanted to be sure to have enough time to meet with Sebrian and still get back home before nightfall, when the air temperature would dip drastically and darkened skies made traveling more dangerous.

He stayed just long enough to refresh his horse and make a quick tour of the building. He made notes about the numerous repairs needed so when reviewing his finances, these could be factored into the balance. With each item listed, his heart grew heavier. How could he have let his father's last and greatest creation fall into such a state? Charles felt ashamed.

Some time later, after riding through more of the divided properties that once belonged to John Marsh, Charles arrived at Sebrian's house. He noticed that even the Sebrian fence-line extended its reach into previous Marsh territory, as the gate announcing entrance to the ranch was at least a mile closer to the Great Stone House than during his earlier visits. This, Charles thought, would have made his father very sad.

Charles knew that Sebrian would invite him in, even without knowing why he was there. They were too connected not to extend that courtesy. It was Charles, after all, that was responsible for tracking down and imprisoning his daughter's husband - a husband that would be absent for the rest of her life.

Charles, however, was never sure how much this truly disturbed Sebrian. He heard that Sebrian never thought very highly of Felipe Moreno, but also knew that he was intensely devoted to his children and their happiness. If his daughter was still upset, then Sebrian would likely direct his anger toward Charles.

But Charles suspected that that was not the only thing connecting the two. If his father's hidden gold did exist and there really was a map stolen by Moreno, then Sebrian would be just as interested in staying in touch with Charles as he was to John Marsh. So it was not surprising when the large wooden door swung open just as Charles stepped onto the porch.

During his visits to the Sebrian home over the years, he could never remember actually making it to the door before it opened. Someone always seemed to know he was coming, or at least saw him approaching. This always made Charles uncomfortable.

Sebrian had aged a great deal in the eleven years since Charles first met him. The perpetual grin had eroded into a stern countenance years ago. His hair had begun to gray and he no longer looked like he rode and worked with the vaqueros as in the past. He looked old, Charles thought; old and worn.

"Señor Marsh, come in. To what do I owe this visit?"

The false pleasantries of Sebrian always bothered Charles, but today, they were particularly unsettling. "Mr. Sebrian, I'd like a few moments of your time to discuss a matter. I've just spent some length of time with Felipe Moreno and wish to speak with you about our conversation."

Sebrian paused with a thoughtful expression. Charles could tell that what he said both intriguing and concerning to Sebrian. "Let us sit. May I offer you a drink?"

"No, thank you."

"Then, please, follow me." Sebrian led Charles to a side room that appeared to be a scaled down version of a study with a desk and high-backed upholstered chairs currently occupied by two individuals. "Let me introduce you to my children. I believe you have met my daughter Isabella."

Charles met the wife of Felipe Moreno in passing at the house in years past and saw her often during the trial, but had never had a conversation with her. He felt extremely uncomfortable with the introduction, assuming that she hated him for her husband's situation. He also assumed that his discomfort was exactly what Sebrian intended. They exchanged greetings, but that was all.

"And this is my son, Navarro." Charles knew about Navarro, but had never met him. According to Sebrian, his son spent most of his time in the south of California arranging business transactions for his father.

"Hello. I'm Charles Marsh," Charles said, looking Navarro directly in the eye, searching for an expression that would reveal true emotions hidden beneath the same fixed smile that his father used to carry.

Navarro appeared to be in his early twenties. He was taller than his father, but still short in stature compared to Charles. When he shook Charles' hand, Charles felt that he gripped it much tighter than necessary, perhaps over compensating for the height difference, or perhaps trying to send an underlying message. Charles was not sure, but it didn't matter.

He was here to talk with Sebrian and so shrugged off Navarro. Both children were directed to leave the room which they did obediently.

"Please sit."

"No, thank you. I prefer to stand at the moment."

"Then what is it I can do for you?"

"What is the real reason you had my father killed?"

The question took even Charles by surprise. He had no intention of being so direct, but for some reason found himself saying exactly what he was thinking. Perhaps he was more confident now that Moreno was behind bars, or perhaps he was just tired of restraint. Whatever the reason, he found himself just as shocked as Sebrian at the question.

Clearly disturbed by the accusation, Sebrian replied, "You walk a very fine line, Señor Marsh. I believe we determined years ago that Felipe acted against your father because he was cheated out of money. I had nothing to do with that." Sebrian then turned his back to Charles and poured himself a drink from a whiskey bottle resting on the desk.

"I determined that Moreno murdered my father for money, alright, but not for the money on his person. Tell me Mr. Sebrian, are you any closer to finding the map that Moreno took than you were eleven years ago when you told him to steal it?"

Charles found his unfamiliar boldness cathartic. It was a relief to say just what he thought and felt and though he was still just as furious, it was extremely satisfying to direct his anger openly at its intended target with no sense of propriety or remorse to dilute it. Charles wasn't sure what he hoped to accomplish with his frankness.

He knew that Sebrian would never confess to being involved in his father's murder, but if he could force a reaction, any reaction that resulted in Sebrian losing his calm, self-assured demeanor, then perhaps it would be worth it. And it appeared to be working.

Sebrian spun around quickly, the whiskey in his glass sloshing over the rim. "I do not know what you are talking about. And I very much resent these continued allegations."

Charles walked directly toward Sebrian. He could feel the tension between the two men growing exponentially with each step. "Neither you nor I have the map that was taken from my father. And neither you nor I know where his gold is. But I will tell you this much…" Charles clenched his jaw and stared into Sebrian's face, "you can search for a hundred years for the map and for the gold, and you will never find them. I swear on my father's grave that you will never find them."

The veins in Sebrian's forehead pulsated as he tried to contain his anger. Ygnacio Sebrian had spent well over eleven years chasing after the John Marsh treasure. He was as frustrated and weary as Charles and the thought that he might spend the rest of his life so close without ever touching it was more than he could suppress – and he exploded!

Sebrian flung his whiskey glass against the wall. The splintered glass sprayed the side of Charles' face. "Enough! Get the hell out of my house! Get the hell off of my property!" He snatched up the half empty whiskey bottle and heaved it toward Charles head. "Out!"

Charles dodged the bottle and sheltered his eyes as it shattered against the wall behind him. Charles' sense of satisfaction at riling Sebrian to this extreme brought an ever-so-slight smile across his face as he ducked out of the way. He turned back toward Sebrian and with as placid an expression as he could create said, "And you, sir, have a good day." Charles swung back around and exited the study.

But before he made his way out, Sebrian called from behind, "I WILL find the map, Señor Marsh. And I WILL find your father's gold!"

Charles froze. The admission ignited the general disdain that Charles had come to have for Sebrian into a fierce hatred. With his heart pounding and his fists clenched tightly, he slowly turned back toward Sebrian, who stood staring fiery-eyed at him. So many thoughts about the past decade flew through Charles' mind that he felt dizzy – his father's burial, the years of searching, the Moreno trial – all of this due to the greed of this one man standing in front of him.

Charles stepped toward Sebrian. He could kill him. He *would* kill him.

"Papa, is everything alright?"

Isabella's voice from the next room was quiet and concerned. It momentarily distracted Charles from his rage. Could she cope without her husband and now, perhaps, without her father? An image of Alice leapt into his mind. He couldn't … he wouldn't kill Sebrian.

But he could *hurt* him.

Charles constricted his right fist as tight as he could and with the force of eleven years of pent up anger - swung! The punch landed squarely on the chin of a stunned Sebrian, lifting him off his feet and launching him backward three feet before his body fell limp and twisted between the two chairs.

Charles stared at the unconscious man on the floor. He'd probably fractured Sebrian's jaw and likely dislodged several teeth – and it felt good. He knew this would never be satisfactory retribution, nothing would. But it was a start.

As Charles left the house, he caught a glimpse of Isabella and Navarro running into the study where their father lay, presumably still unconscious and definitely injured. Charles had to accept the sense of relief, as moderate as it was, that came from assuming Sebrian had to give up his search for the John Marsh gold, knowing that Charles was now fully aware of his involvement.

Perhaps, Charles reasoned, I will never find the gold – but at least no one else will.

CHAPTER 27

THE WARNING BELL FOR FIRST PERIOD rang while Celeste finished preparing her lessons. She rested her coffee on the desk and quickly began sifting through e-mails. As was typical, she tried to get through as many messages as possible before class started, finishing the rest during her prep period or after school.

She opened one that just popped up from the clerk who coordinated substitute teachers and instinctively gasped – 'sub needed for Harrison Barrett'. Celeste quickly called the office.

"Hi, Jeanine, this is Celeste. Do you know why Harrison is out today?"

"No, I don't. But there's a line of kids at his room with no teacher."

"You mean he didn't call in for a sub?"

"No."

"That's strange, isn't it?"

"Very strange for him. He's usually very responsible in notifying us if he's not going to be in; whether sick, flat tire, whatever. He's not answering his phone, either. Not sure what the problem is, but we'll cover his class and hopefully he'll show up soon."

"Thanks, Jeanine." Celeste hung up the phone and a wave of anxiety washed over her. This was not at all like Harrison. Something was wrong, she could sense it. But what? Where could he be?

Celeste did her best to regain her composure while students flooded into the classroom. She would, for now, have to purge her mind of any thoughts of trouble so she could concentrate on her job. He must have just overslept or wasn't feeling well and forgot to call in. In any case, she'd check back with the office or call his house during lunch to get an update.

"Good morning, Ms. Scott."

The greeting from a student jolted her back to the business at hand.

"Good morning," Celeste replied with a smile.

THE DUCT TAPE THAT BOUND Harrison's feet and hands was beginning to create extreme discomfort. He had been forced to bind his own ankles while a gun was pointed at his head and, unfortunately, did an excellent job. The curly-haired man made Harrison lie down while he wrapped his wrists behind his back. Harrison managed to roll over onto his back, but that was at least three hours ago and his joints now ached intensely.

Harrison knew exactly where he was. When they left the Vasco Caves area, the curly-haired man sat in the back seat of Harrison's car while forcing him to drive. Thirty minutes later, in the dim light of dawn, they pulled into a house set back on a deserted ranch property. As they walked toward the front door, it was obvious this was a vacated foreclosure, with the telltale weed infested front yard, bank sign on the window, and lock box attached to the front door handle.

The Brentwood community was hit particularly hard with the recession and foreclosed homes in various states of disrepair were scattered throughout the city. Harrison found himself impressed with the curly-haired man's hideout location. It was near enough to town, yet far away enough from potentially prying neighbors. It would be sheer coincidence if anyone actually came to check on the property during the time he squatted in it. And by entering through a kicked-in side door, no one would notice the house being used.

Harrison regularly adjusted his position, trying to prevent the blood from pooling in one limb or the other. At one point, while the curly-haired man stepped into the kitchen, Harrison managed to squirm along the floor to the nearest wall and at least prop upright against it.

When the man returned with a beer in hand, he clearly noticed the relocation, but chose to ignore it, apparently feeling that Harrison was no threat to escape in his current condition.

"So, what's our next move?" Harrison asked hoping, once again, that engaging his captor in conversation was his best chance at altering his present circumstance.

The curly-haired man turned from where he was seated across the room. "After night fall, we'll return to dig some more."

And what if, thought Harrison, nothing was found tonight either – which he figured was a definite possibility? There had to be something else. Something that was missing from the clues that he and Celeste had found.

"Do you have the original document that you stole from the Moreno's home?" Harrison was extremely nervous about asking so blatant a question. He was very uncertain how the curly-haired man would react.

There was a long pause as the question was considered. "Why?"

"Can I look at it? All I have is a copy. Maybe there's something wrong with it."

No response.

"Look," Harrison continued, "I don't care if I find gold or not. Personally, I don't even think there is any. But *if* there is, and I can help find it so you'll be on your way, then at least let me try."

The curly-haired man took a long drink from his beer and sat it firmly on the table. He got up and left the room without saying a word. A moment later, he returned, unrolled a paper and laid it on the floor next to his hostage. Harrison instantly recognized the paper as the old document that had previously hung on the wall of Alex Moreno's home.

He studied it acutely; his eyes examining every detail. The diagram of the bird appeared exactly the same as young Gabrielle had drawn it – a cigar shaped body crossed by another thin oval representing wings and outlined by numerous short lines portraying feathers.

Each word was spelled exactly as he remembered from the copy. It was possible that the translation he and Celeste arrived at was wrong. He was also quite aware of the inherent error in determining exactly how long a 'step' was.

For a moment, his mind wandered to his early years of teaching science when he often had students demonstrate the need for standardizing measurements by having them measure distances in feet – *their* feet. It always brought the point home when the same distance was reported as various quantities depending on the shoe size of the measurer. He wondered why John Marsh did not use a standard measurement for the distances and conjectured that it was probably intentional.

The only difference Harrison noticed on the original map was the existence of several circles surrounding the bird figure. He did not recall these being on the copy. Five circles of varying sizes, two clustered to the left, two clustered to the right, and one slightly higher and off-center from the others.

The more he pondered the circles, the more he felt that they were not random images. There had to be a purpose to them. Why else would they be included on such an important document? But why were they there? What did they represent? Harrison was baffled. The discomfort from his bindings made it difficult for him to concentrate for long, so he leaned his head back against the wall and closed his eyes.

CELESTE LEFT SCHOOL IMMEDIATELY after the last period. She raced home to change her clothes, then headed toward the Vasco Caves Regional Preserve. If she was right, Harrison was not at school because he decided to try to locate the gold on his own. The afternoon was warm, but she made good time during the hike to the vernal pools. This is where he would start looking, she thought, the place of the 'disappearing water'.

Caves were visible in all directions, but she chose to begin with the ones closest to the pools, deducing that Harrison would also be methodical in his search. To her surprise, the first set of caves had a painting that resembled the bird image. But she searched for half an hour without finding any evidence that Harrison had been there.

After moving to a second set of caves that had no paintings at all, she hiked to a third set. Immediately she sensed that the area had been disturbed. It appeared like the soil was recently trampled.

Within a few moments of walking the area, the evidence of a large hole became obvious. There was no doubt in her mind that this was Harrison's work. She searched the surrounding site intensely, looking for anything that might indicate what had happened or where he might be. She found a second hole, but nothing else meaningful.

Frustrated, and worried, Celeste retraced her steps back toward the interior of the cave and the bird image – and then she noticed it – the writing below the bird was faint and decidedly not ancient looking. She knelt down close and traced her fingers along the letters.

'W-I-T-O-K-A'. She thought for a moment ... and then gasped. She remembered what the word meant from the practice translations she and Harrison had done on the Internet.

"Oh, shit..." Celeste said quietly to herself, "... *male captive*."

CHAPTER XXVIII

June 4, 1867

IT TOOK CHARLES TWO DAYS by horse and buggy to cover the sixty mile journey from the Great Stone House in Brentwood to Mrs. Thomson's home in Oakland. Anxious to see Alice, he urged the tired horse to a quick trot while still several miles away.

He had not seen her for nearly a year. She grew and changed so much between visits that he stopped trying to predict her appearance and knew the only thing consistent would be the bright blue eyes. Her golden blonde had darkened as she matured, but those blue eyes would still be as vivid as ever.

In his mind, she was still the bubbly four-year old that was first introduced as his sister well over a decade ago, though the last time he was with her, he couldn't help but admire the beautiful, articulate young lady she had become, and he was all the more eager to see how much more she had matured since then.

With a refreshing, cool breeze blowing in off the bay, the temperature in Oakland was at least twenty degrees cooler than the previous day. Charles was thankful for some relief from the stifling temperatures further inland, particularly since the tale he was about to tell Alice made him nervous enough without the added stress of summer heat.

Charles reasoned it was time to explain the whole story of her father's death to Alice. Why he was murdered. Who was responsible. What the murderers were after. Thus far, Alice knew only the public version of a disgruntled employee who ambushed and killed John Marsh over a wage dispute. By the end of the day, however, she would know much more.

This was only part of the angst with which he struggled. He also had to tell her about the house … the Great Stone House. He was convinced that he had tried everything and sought advice from everyone, but to no avail. There was no way they could keep the Great Stone House.

His father's savings were spent years ago, and what was left of the ranch that still carried the Marsh name just couldn't turn a profit, and had, in fact, been operating in the red for so long that Charles had to borrow from Alice's inheritance to pay off debts. But he could not stand to do this any longer.

The arrangements were already made. Charles just needed a signature from Alice to finalize the transaction that would forever end the Marsh family's claim over Rancho Los Meganos and the magnificent Stone House.

As he sat in the parlor awaiting the lemonade that Mrs. Thomson was preparing, he found himself staring at Alice as she sat in an opposing chair, one leg tucked under her, looking young and vibrant. He noticed the long, floral print dress she wore was the exact shade of blue as her eyes and wondered whether this was intentional. She talked rapidly about work around the home, school, and even boys. Charles listened intently, enraptured by his sister's exuberance.

For two hours or more, they shared stories about life over the past year. Charles was especially interested in hearing about the visit from James Marsh, their father's brother, who traveled from back east to Oakland to visit his niece. Charles, regretfully, was out of the area during this time, and insisted that Alice recount every detail about their uncle.

Finally, the time Charles dreaded came. He must begin describing the tale of their father's death and his quest for justice.

"Come, Alice. Let's walk," Charles said. "I have an important story to tell you."

Alice looked puzzled, but was more than ready to get up and move, since they had been sitting for quite a while.

"Do you remember how our father died?" Charles continued.

"Of course. He was killed by one of his workers on September 24, 1856, thirteen years ago...by the man that you caught a few years back."

"Quite right," Charles replied, impressed by her knowledge of the details. "But do you know why?"

"He thought father owed him money, even though he didn't do the work he was hired to do."

"It turns out, Alice, that there's more to it than that. Much more..."

Charles and his sister strolled slowly along paths that meandered through the outskirts of Oakland where Mrs. Thomson's home nestled in between oak trees and an apple orchard. He recounted the events as he uncovered them; from the actions of Felipe Moreno, to the directive given by Ygnacio Sebrian, to the ultimate motive for it all ... gold.

Charles watched as Alice soaked it all in. She was clearly in shock.

"Gold? Buried on our property? How is that possible? Where could it be?"

Charles stopped under the shade of a large oak tree, whose century old branches extended outward forming a canopy that provided protective cover. They sat on a large fallen branch while Alice continued to puzzle over the revelation.

"And that, my dearest sister, is perhaps the saddest story of all. It is no longer our property."

"What do you mean?"

Charles had always believed that Alice did not have a strong emotional connection to the ranch and the house, but was never certain. She did spend the early years of her life there with her father and seemed very content when he first met her. But after John Marsh died, Alice appeared to gradually lose interest in the things she once loved to do: play in the stone tower, visit the Indian village, or ride her pony through the orchards. So Charles assumed ... he hoped ... that she wouldn't miss it.

"We must sell what remains of the Marsh ranch ... including the house. I'm afraid we just cannot afford to run the property or care for the stone house anymore. I've already made arrangements. I'll just need you to sign the deed of sale. It breaks my heart to have to do this, but we have no other choice."

Alice sat quietly, her eyes focused on the dried grass beneath her shoes.

"Well? How are you feeling about all this?" Charles finally asked.

"I'm not sure. Sad. Confused, I suppose."

"I understand. What can I do to help?"

"We are out of money, and so must sell the rest of father's property, yet there may be thousands of dollars' worth of gold on this same property..."

"I'm afraid that's correct, as ironic as it sounds."

234

"Will you keep looking for the gold?"

"Heavens no. Sebrian and Moreno have been searching for many, many years and turned up nothing. While there might be gold, I am convinced that it will never be found. Besides, I am through with that chapter of my life. I *must* be through with it. I have to finally put father's death and everything associated with it behind me so I can begin to live my own life."

"What will you do?"

"I am considering heading back to Sacramento to look for work."

The two sat in silence for some time, staring out into the countryside, listening to the occasional call of a nearby crow. Alice finally interrupted the quiet with a question.

"Charles?" she said turning toward him, "What if *I* want to look for the gold?"

Charles looked into his sister's vibrant blue eyes and replied, "I wondered if you might be interested ..." He dug into the leather satchel that he brought along and pulled out a book. It was, in fact, the journal of John Marsh; the one his father had given to him just prior to his murder. Charles had retrieved it from Mrs. Thomson many years earlier in an attempt to once again uncover its hidden meaning – to no avail.

"This, my dear sister, is all I can offer."

As Alice flipped through the leather-bound volume, it was clear to Charles that she was now inspecting the journal very differently than she ever would have done when it was previously in her possession.

"Are you telling me there are clues in this that lead to father's gold?"

"Father never had a chance to say specifically, but that is what I believe to be true. However, the journal may be incomplete – with a page missing here or there, like the one that Felipe Moreno stole that contains important information. But it is yours to keep and do with what you will. I no longer have a need for it."

Alice closed the cover of the book. She sighed, hooked her arm around his and laid her head onto his shoulder. Charles laid his head on hers and they sat, silently, Charles lost in thoughts of the past and Alice engrossed by thoughts of the future.

Alice Marsh Camron[13]

CHAPTER 29

HIS MUSCLES ACHED FROM THE HOURS of being bound and motionless, nonetheless, Harrison was glad to be hiking the trail back to Vasco Caves. Even the added weight of the pick and shovel he was again carrying didn't discount the feeling that he would rather be moving with a man ten feet behind pointing a gun at his back than taped up lying on a floor.

He knew it was late at night, but wasn't sure exactly what time it was. The moon was still bright enough to cover the hills in a dim glow that provided plenty of light to see the trail and nearby surroundings.

Harrison knew his predicament was dire. If no gold was found this night, he felt certain that the curly-haired man would feel no further need for his help … or for him.

Plots for escape raced through his mind with each turn in the trail. He considered every possible way to attack and disarm his captor. But nothing he could think of was practical, or even plausible enough to attempt. And so, for now, he would bide his time and willingly participate one last time in the expedition to locate the John Marsh treasure.

During the trek, Harrison's thoughts were interspersed with another worry that added significantly to his anxiety. He had already followed every clue he was aware of and was unsuccessful. Why would tonight be any different? How many more caves with bird pictographs could he possibly locate and dig up prior to dawn? And the worst possibility of all – what if there never was buried gold in the first place?

The two men approached an area that Harrison was now becoming very familiar with – Vasco Caves. The large rocky outcrops reflected much more of the moonlight than the surrounding soil and appeared almost fluorescent in the night. Harrison began a visual search for the two caves at which he had already dug and as he scanned the hillsides – he tripped, falling hard on his chest; the added weight of the pick and shovel increasing the force by which he landed.

"Goddamnit!"

The curly-haired man said nothing, but Harrison could tell by his body language that he was suspicious this might be some kind of get-away attempt. Harrison pulled himself onto his feet, brushed off his shirt and bent down to retrieve the pickaxe he released as he fell. While doing so, he instinctively turned and looked down at the ground to locate the object that he stumbled over.

It was a concretion, one of the near perfectly round half-spheres protruding up from the underlying substrate. Harrison's science background automatically compelled him to think back to the explanation given by Ranger Rick about the formation of these objects – and why their presence made this area so unique.

And then it hit him … almost as hard as the impact of the ground when he tripped. Concretions. The unique round objects protruding from the ground – and from rock walls.

Harrison immediately forgot about his circumstance and turned excitedly to the curly-haired man, "The map. Let me see the original map. Quickly!"

The curly-haired man did not move, unsure what had just happened and still highly suspicious of Harrison's motives. After quiet consideration, he slowly pulled the map from a pouch he carried while keeping his eyes – and gun – focused carefully on Harrison. He tossed the map. Harrison caught it out of the air and quickly unfolded it. He turned the map and held it up to allow the moonlight to illuminate the drawing and after just a few seconds of intense examination, exclaimed, "That's it. That has to be it."

The curly-haired man finally broke his silence. "What's it? What have you found?"

"The markers." Harrison replied. "The markers for the cave."

"What are you talking about?"

"Clever son-of-a-bitch, that John Marsh. Look …" In Harrison's giddy enthusiasm, he forgot all about his precarious situation, and so walked straight toward the curly-haired man with the map outstretched.

"Stop now!"

Harrison froze, momentarily drawn back to his predicament by the too familiar sound of the pistol hammer drawing back. But a moment later he was overcome, "Look … here on the drawing … the bird pictograph is surrounded by these odd circles. Why?"

The curly-haired man now seemed to believe that Harrison's antics were not just some distraction to get him to lower his guard. He stepped back a few paces and pulled out a flashlight, shining it onto the map. "Explain."

"John Marsh knew that there were many of these bird pictographs scattered all over the hills around here. He probably also knew that those Indian cave drawings wouldn't last forever. So, he added another indicator. One that had already lasted for

240

thousands of years and would last for thousands more ... the concretions."

"What the hell is a cretion?"

"Con–cretion ... this." Harrison pointed down at the half-sphere imbedded in the ground that he tripped over moments ago.

"And what does this have to do with the gold?"

Harrison now became annoyed that his captor, holding a gun pointed directly at his chest, was not quick enough to follow along. "These circles surrounding the image of a bird – they have to represent concretions outside of a cave – the cave that is the starting point for pacing off the steps to the treasure."

"So if we find a cave that has those con ... whatever there are, that match the drawing, then we'll find the gold?"

"Exactly. Now let's get moving."

Harrison again entirely forgot about the captor-captive relationship that he had with the curly-haired man. He was now engrossed with a laser-like focus on locating the cave whose exterior concretions matched the relative size and placement of those on the drawing.

The curly-haired man had difficulty keeping up with Harrison's quick pace, especially since he was still limping badly. They bypassed the two caves that were nearest the vernal pools - the two that Harrison had already explored – and for the first time Harrison noticed the concretions.

The first cave had just one and the second cave and several that were visible, but they were not at all similar in design to the map. Harrison was feeling more and more confident in his hypothesis about the meaning of the circles. His excitement grew as he again scanned the hillsides for rock formations and then locked onto one on the opposite side of the vernal pools.

Off again Harrison dashed toward the next likely outcrop, still too far away to tell in the dim light whether there were concretions, or even a cave.

"Slow down. Now!" the curly-haired man yelled, fearing that Harrison was getting too far ahead to be in range of his weapon.

Harrison obliged, but with difficulty, as his inquisitive nature was clearly getting the better of him.

Within a few dozen yards of the formation, the gaping entrance to a large cave became visible; and a few yards closer, Harrison could begin to make out the appearance of round structures imbedded in the wall surrounding the opening. His pulse began to race as he unfolded the stolen document he was still carrying.

Five circles on the drawing. Five concretions imbedded in the wall. Two circles to the left, two to the right, and one above and off center from the cave opening . . . and the concretions matched exactly. Even their relative sizes were similar to the drawing.

Harrison could hardly believe what he was seeing. The only thing missing was the actual bird pictograph. He began to cautiously enter the cave, the curly-haired man now just a few feet behind. Harrison felt his heart pounding with anticipation . . . until he realized after entering the cave that he couldn't see a thing, much less a faint thousand year old painting.

"A flashlight. Quick, gimme a flashlight!"

The curly-haired man hesitated only briefly before tossing the light to Harrison who caught it and immediately illuminated the back of the cave wall.

...and there it was. The rust tinted image was set amidst a variety of geometric designs and other colorations, but it was clear. The cylindrical body with outstretched wings jumped out at Harrison as if it had flown off its centuries old perch.

For a moment he thought about not saying anything to the curly-haired man, but this passed quickly. If gold could be found, perhaps this ordeal could finally end with no one else getting hurt ... perhaps.

CHAPTER XXX

March 7, 1891

M*y Dearest Alice,*

It is outrageous. Completely and utterly outrageous.

Surely, you have heard by now of the governor's pardon of that murderer, Felipe Moreno. I returned to Sacramento as soon as I received word; however, I was too late.

The only details I was given was that a lawyer convinced the governor that Moreno was convicted based only on the hearsay testimony of another man and no real evidence had been presented. And since he had already spent twenty-five years in prison, the just thing to do would be to free him.

My feeling, however, is that the just thing to do would be to hang him as should have been done twenty-five years ago, when I captured him.

Forgive my harsh words, sister, but I am most frustrated by this turn of events. Recounting the memories of the ten years of my life lost to pursuing retribution for our father has been very painful.

To have that man free again to see his family and live his life is almost unbearable. I shall continue to seek advice, both legal and political, that might suggest a way to overturn this injustice.

I shall keep you informed.
As always, yours,
Charles

The letter was addressed to Alice Camron of Oakland. Alice had married William Walker Camron when she turned nineteen and was now raising their daughter, Amy, in a large Victorian house built on the shores of Lake Merritt using much of the remainder of her inheritance from her father's death, thirty-five years prior.

Alice and Charles seldom saw each other. Alice was busy with a family of her own and Charles spent much of his time out of the area, typically in Los Angeles seeking a variety of business opportunities, with which he always struggled. Alice's husband also had difficulties with finances. Without her inheritance, they too would have found life difficult.

As it was, the marriage was shaky, at best. Alice found herself and Amy alone quite often, as William spent days or weeks away at a time pursuing a variety of ventures, including land use investment and politics, all of them ultimately fruitless.

She never mentioned the existence, or possible existence, of her father's gold for fear that William would grow obsessed with trying to find it. A fear that was founded from past experience with his schemes.

In fact, Alice seldom thought about the gold. Every once in a while, when finances were particularly tough or she felt especially distant from her husband, she considered digging up her father's old journal, now stored unceremoniously in a box somewhere in the attic. But the desire would quickly fade as she clung to her present reality and dispelled thoughts of an uncertain future.

So, for now and the foreseeable future, Dr. John Marsh's journal remained hidden away in the Camron's attic on the shores of Lake Merritt in the middle of Oakland. Any secrets contained within would remain concealed and unknown to the world, perhaps forever.

THE REUNION OF FELIPE MORENO with his family was not as joyful a celebration as one might expect. It was, in fact, quite somber. Moreno was fifty-five years of age now, but his body portrayed that of a much older man. He was thin and worn. With nearly half his life spent incarcerated, his body aged beyond its years.

The journey from northern California's San Quentin prison outside of San Francisco to the home of his wife, Isabella Sebrian, in Santa Barbara County to the south, was long and arduous, made longer by an imperative detour through the hills of Martinez.

When he finally arrived at the house, the woman who met him at the door barely recognized him; and he her. Moreno had not seen Isabella in at least two years, perhaps more; it was difficult to remember. They exchanged a few letters throughout the year, but that was it.

He had written of his pending release, but wasn't sure whether she received the notice. Judging by the lack of surprise on her face, she had. But it was difficult to tell whether she was actually happy to see him or, more importantly, to have him back in her life.

It was the man standing behind his wife in the doorway; however, that most caught Moreno's attention. Their son, Alfredo, was born during the time Moreno was on the run following John Marsh's murder. And after his capture, Isabella rarely brought Alfredo to visit his father. So the sight of this grown man was both startling and pleasing.

Moreno carefully studied his son's features, now in his thirties. Although his son's face had matured and filled out, he was still recognizable. Most telling was the curly black hair, a trait shared by his mother, Isabella, and her father, Ygnacio Sebrian.

Moreno shook hands with Alfredo, as two men might that recognize each other, but are not quite sure from where. As Moreno dragged his weary body into the modest home, Alfredo immediately introduced him to his wife and four children, two of them appeared to be teenagers and all with the same curly black hair as their father.

For the next several hours, the family exchanged pleasantries and filled Moreno in on the lives of his son and grandchildren. But during this time, there was an important matter that distracted Moreno from fully absorbing or appreciating the conversation. He knew that he would not be truly at ease until he brought resolution to this matter.

But now was not the time. After dinner, he thought, would be a better time to speak with his son without others knowing.

The evening meal nearly brought tears to Moreno. Isabella prepared tortillas with seasoned rice and beans and the flavors instantly transported him back to a childhood that was long forgotten. Following dinner, Moreno felt the time had come to talk with his son.

"Alfredo, my son, please sit with me outside. I have something to discuss with you."

"Yes, of course." Alfredo was not yet comfortable calling this man father, and wasn't sure whether he would ever be, so for now, he didn't call him anything.

The two men headed toward a shed on the edge of the property. The sun was low in the sky, but there was still plenty of light. They sat on hay bales and Moreno reached into the satchel he brought along and pulled out a large folded paper.

"What is that?" asked Alfredo.

"This ... it is the most valuable thing I own. It is why I went to prison. And it is why I am here with you now."

"I don't understand."

Moreno unfolded the paper and laid it out on the ground so both men could study it. On the paper was a drawing of a bird, surrounded by some circles with words below in an unfamiliar language.

"I still don't understand," Alfredo continued. "What is it?"

"It is ... a map," responded Moreno. "A map to a fortune in gold. I am much too old and tired to search for it now. But you ... you, my son, could find it. This map was hidden away for over thirty years. I retrieved it before coming here because I wanted to give it to you. You can be the one to figure out how to read it and to find the gold. You can be the one to bring riches to our family. You can make all my years spent in prison worth something."

Alfredo sat silent and perplexed for several minutes, contemplating what he had just been told. "And what if ... what if I cannot find this gold?"

"Then you must pass the information on to your son. And he will pass it on to his. One day, a Moreno will discover its secret and we will all be free to live the life that we deserve."

Alfredo did not quite follow his father's reasoning, but he was thoroughly intrigued. "I will keep this paper safe. Perhaps framed and displayed with prominence, so that all in our family will know of its importance, even though they will not all know its meaning. You must tell me the whole story. All of what you know about the gold and where it might be. And one day, we will find this treasure and the Morenos will be wealthy. And that will be due to you ... Father."

CHAPTER 31

THE COYOTES YELPING NEARBY went unnoticed as Harrison dashed toward the bird painting, turned his back to the cave wall and started counting off steps. By now, the number and direction of the paces as described in the Moreno's framed document were etched into his mind.

Thirteen Steps West. Harrison quickly but precisely marked off the steps according to the reading on the compass surrendered to him by the curly-haired man.

He then carefully turned to his left and took eight steps toward the south and found himself just outside the cave entrance. He adjusted the compass and redirected his body back toward the west.

The anticipation of walking off the final sixteen steps had Harrison's blood racing through his veins. He inhaled deeply, again oblivious to the weapon tracking his every move. "Fourteen ... fifteen ... sixteen ..."

Harrison stared at the ground, examining it as if expecting a huge X to be somehow imprinted into the dirt. But there was nothing. Nothing that over one-hundred and fifty years of weathering and erosion wouldn't have covered or destroyed.

He shined the flashlight in all directions, looking for anything out of the ordinary, but found no indication that this particular spot was any different than ten feet to the left or right. And yet, this is where the clues had led him, and this is where he must dig.

With that realization, an intense feeling of anxiety washed over him. If there were no treasure underneath his feet, which was a definite possibility, this could be his last moments alive. He glanced behind him at the curly-haired man, now standing just a few yards away. Still too far to make a successful lunge without the likelihood of being shot. "A better time will come," Harrison thought, "... a better time *has* to come."

The foreboding in which Harrison was awash was suddenly dissipated by a voice, "Start digging. Start digging, now!"

Harrison shook off his fear and collected his thoughts. He dropped his backpack onto the ground and lifted the pickaxe. He hoisted it high above his head ... then swung it hard onto the ground.

The soil was not soft, but it was not terribly hard and compacted either. Each swing of the pick loosened a significant chunk of dirt. After a few swings, Harrison traded the pick for a shovel and began removing the dirt, tossing it far to the side.

As he continued, his mind started calculating again ... the curly-haired man looked tired from the hike on his bad leg. It would be better to attempt something before he fully rested. In addition, if Harrison kept digging, his own fatigue would grow, making him less effective.

But he needed to draw the man closer. Perhaps again trying to engage in conversation would lower his guard, even just slightly, to a point where his odds improved enough to risk an escape attempt.

"What I still don't understand," Harrison announced, "is how you knew about the existence of the document in the Moreno house."

Harrison continued digging, hoping his question appeared innocuous and that the curly-haired man would see no harm in explaining. The delay was long. Harrison excavated a dozen shovelfuls of soil while his captor pondered an answer.

Then, finally. "My father told me about the map. From the time I was a young boy in Mexico, he told the story of a treasure of gold that would make our family rich.

Harrison was surprised to hear a response, but grateful for it. "How did your father know about it?"

There was another pause, this time shorter. "My father was told by his father. The story has been passed down for many years."

"But how did you know it was at the Moreno's house?"

There was no delay in the curly-haired man's answer this time and Harrison detected an air of confidence growing in his response, which was good, he thought. The cockier he grew, the more likely he'd relax his guard.

"We always knew it was in the hands of a Moreno, but did not know which Moreno. There are a lot. I have spent many, many years looking for the right one. When I found a family in this city, I asked a boy in the family if he recognized the drawing of the bird, and he said, yes."

At the mention of 'a boy', Harrison's senses amplified. He realized, almost shamefully, that in the midst of his own turmoil during the past few days he had lost focus on how he became involved in this ordeal in the first place – the death of Alex Moreno. But now, with the curly-haired man specifically referencing Alex, Harrison grew furious.

He increased the pace and force of the pick swings and flung the dislodged soil further to the edges. He knew he was losing strength with each pound of the pick, but was not yet ready to act against his captor.

The hole was now four feet in diameter and at least two feet deep. Harrison stopped digging momentarily to wipe his face. As he lifted the pick and began swinging again he asked, "So what is your name?" Harrison was hoping the curly-haired man's arrogance in being in control of the situation would continue to loosen his tongue … and it did.

"Sebrian. Javier Sebrian."

"Well, Javier Sebrian. What happens if there's no gold in this hole I'm digging?"

"That's easy," Sebrian replied, "you die."

Though Harrison's heart was pulsing with fear, he did his best to present a calm response, "Yeah, that's pretty much what I thought. So tell me, then, why'd you kill the boy?"

Again Harrison knew he was walking a thin line with his questioning but since Sebrian had already confirmed his plans, he figured he would try to get the whole story in case, by some miracle, he found a way out of his plight.

"I told the boy I would buy the map from him. I would have just paid him the money and taken the map, but when he showed up that night, he decided he wanted more money. Told me a story about needing it for college, as if I would care. He tried to leave, but I stopped him. We fought and I hit him and took the map. As I was leaving, he attacked me and I hit him again and knocked him onto the train tracks. It was unfortunate that a train was coming but it was better for me. No loose ends."

Harrison grimaced at the callousness with which Sebrian told the story, and the rage within him intensified. He launched a mound of dirt and thrust the shovel into the ground, then paused, this time staring directly at Sebrian, "He was just a boy. You didn't need to kill him."

253

It was now obvious to Sebrian that Harrison was enraged. He held the gun high and pointed directly at Harrison's head. "The Sebrian family searched for too many years to let that map get away. I would do anything to get it – and I did. Now keep digging."

Sebrian family. It was the combination of those two terms that triggered the recollection for Harrison. He knew that name. It was unusual and he was sure he heard it before … and not long ago. As Harrison swung the pick again, it came to him – Sebrian was a man in the tale about the death of John Marsh.

He and Celeste read the articles and letters and even the Marsh journal that mentioned a man named Sebrian. A man that Marsh had been in conflict with and that was, in fact, the father-in-law of the convicted murderer.

Harrison thought back to the visit at the Moreno's home when Celeste translated the Moreno family tree. Ygnacio Sebrian was the father-in-law of Felipe Moreno, who in turn was Alex's great, great, great, grandfather. And the curly-haired man standing a few feet away from him, whose ancestors knew about the map, was also named Sebrian. There was no possible way it could be a coincidence. This man was also a descendent of Ygnacio Sebrian. Harrison filtered through the scenarios in his mind while swinging and shoveling. Then abruptly stopped.

It was almost a smile that crossed his face. Not a smile of joy, but rather one of utter astonishment at the irony he had just uncovered.

"Why are you stopping?"

"Because your great, great, great, grandfather was a man named Ygnacio Sebrian."

"Perhaps. I might have heard the name. So what?"

"The 'so what' is that he was also an ancestor of Alex Moreno."

"I don't understand what you're talking about."

Harrison, now dumbfounded and frustrated, slumped down on the rim of the hole and turned toward the curly-haired man, "The man whose gold you're looking for, John Marsh, was murdered by a man named Felipe Moreno; the boy's great, great, great grandfather. And Felipe's father-in-law was Ygnacio Sebrian. Who is also *your* relative."

Sebrian stared at Harrison, still appearing confused about the connection.

"Don't you get it, you son of a bitch? When you killed Alex Moreno that night ... you killed your own cousin."

Sebrian was clearly shocked. He stood motionless, mouth agape and eyes wide at this revelation.

"For all these years you've been trying to find this gold to help out your family, only to find out that in doing so, you killed a member *of* your own family."

"Shut up!" Sebrian shouted, now awakened from his stupor. "Shut up and keep digging."

Harrison, thoroughly exhausted, slowly grabbed the pick, lifted it, and let gravity drag it down into the soil. But something was different when it landed. Rather than the heavy iron head sinking deep into the ground, it stopped suddenly and stuck. Harrison at first figured it must be a root, but after scanning his surroundings, realized there wasn't a tree or shrub nearby.

He gently pried the pick from the dirt. This time, lifting it high and swinging it with great effort, the pick landed. Again it stuck. The sound was clearly different – not soil and not rock. Harrison wondered whether the curly-haired man noticed the contrast, and judging by how close he was now perched to the hole, it was evident that he did.

The pick was quickly exchanged for a shovel and Harrison started scraping off the thin layer of soil that covered the object buried just under the three foot deep hole in which he stood. Once again, the excitement of discovery overcame him and he rapidly unearthed what was clearly wood, old and weathered, and more astonishingly, obviously man-made.

A huge lump formed in Harrison's throat. He continued to rapidly scoop and scrape dirt away from the structure until finally tossing the shovel outside of the ditch and kneeling down to use his hands. An outline took shape of what was without a doubt … a chest. Even the metal hinges were becoming apparent and Harrison was in sheer disbelief of the object beneath him, as if he were uncovering the preserved remains of some mythical creature. He knew what it was, but had a difficult time believing it was real.

After another few minutes, the top three or four inches all the way around the chest were uncovered and a separate hole surrounding the latch was dug out. Harrison excitedly reached for the latch … and then paused.

The curly-haired man, Javier Sebrian, stood crouched at the side of the ditch, just a few feet away from him, a flashlight in one hand and a pistol in the other. The hand holding the gun was lowered, pointing at nothing in particular. He was vulnerable. And Harrison knew that if he was ever to catch the man off guard, this was the time.

If only he had not tossed the shovel outside of the hole, Harrison thought, he would have a perfect weapon. But now all he had were his hands - and a lot of dirt. Harrison took one more scrape of soil along the outline of the chest, but this time he clenched it firmly in his left palm.

Calculating the next moves would be critical. Dirt to the eyes to disorient. A backhand to the bridge of the nose to stun, then a lunge and grasp of the gun hand to disarm. Harrison's only problem, he reasoned, was that he was standing nearly four feet deep in a hole, so his mobility and reach were extremely limited. If Sebrian reacted any differently than anticipated, Harrison knew that he might not be able to reach the gun. But now was the time to try.

Harrison knelt down, pretending to reach for the latch of the chest. From the corner of his eye, he waited for Sebrian to bend a bit closer …

The dirt landed directly in Sebrian's face, forcing him to wince and recoil.

The backhand strike was quick and direct on the top of his nose and Harrison knew the blow had the desired effect of stunning the senses.

But the next move, the critical grasping of the gun hand, did not play out as anticipated. The force of the hit sent Sebrian flailing backward further than Harrison hoped, and as he lunged for the gun, it was out of reach. Harrison was only able the grab the thigh of his captor as he scrambled to get out of the hole.

Sebrian scurried backward, still impaired from the first maneuvers, though he quickly regained sense enough to remember he was holding a gun.

Harrison stretched for the weapon, but it was too far away. Sebrian angled his gun hand toward his attacker and fired.

The bullet buzzed by Harrison's head as he rolled off of Sebrian's legs and in the same motion dashed for the cover of a nearby bolder.

Another shot hit the rock, spraying dust into Harrison's face while he leapt behind it.

Harrison instantly knew he was in a perilous predicament. As soon as Sebrian regained his complete sight and sense, Harrison would be utterly defenseless.

Sebrian rubbed his eyes, clearing the dirt and tears, and got to his feet. He took a step toward the bolder that Harrison now crouched behind, less than thirty feet away. The acutely audible sound of the gun hammer cocking made Harrison turn pale.

There was nowhere else to hide.

CHAPTER 32

THE SITUATION WAS DIRE. Harrison's thoughts, the ones he reasoned would be his last, surprised him. He briefly reflected on his family and how much he would miss them, and on regrets about things he hoped to do and see in his life. But more than anything his mind fixated on the past months spent with Celeste.

It was only now that he realized their relationship meant much more to him than just friendship. He felt more connected to her than he had to any other woman ... ever. The thought of never having the chance to tell her how he felt sickened him.

With Sebrian approaching, Harrison knew he had to act. His mind considered just two possibilities; charge the curly-haired man and attempt to disarm him, or make a run for it. In either scenario, he reasoned, there was a good chance he would be shot.

His hope was that any injury - or injuries - would be minor enough for him to follow through. But that would be pure chance. Of the two options, Harrison decided his best bet would be to flee. He knew that if he could get out of range without being killed, Sebrian's bad leg would prevent him from pursuing.

Sebrian, and his gun, were now just a few feet away on the other side of the rock, so Harrison crouched into a sprinter's stance, took a deep breath ...

"Police! Drop your weapon!"

The voice came from thirty, maybe forty yards away. At first, Harrison thought it was a hallucination, brought on by the stress of realizing he could be about to die. He remained motionless, trying to clear his head.

"I said, drop the weapon, now!"

This time Harrison was sure. It was a real voice. Cautiously, he raised his head from behind the bolder to assess the scene. To his dismay, at least eight bright lights were illuminating the area, all focusing their beams onto the curly-haired man, who Harrison could now clearly see scowling in his direction, gun raised high.

Then finally, after what felt to Harrison like an eternity but was likely just a few seconds, Sebrian lowered his gun hand and released the pistol, allowing it to fall into the dirt.

Another command was shouted out from the dark. "Put your hands on your head."

This time, Sebrian did immediately as instructed. Instantly, a half dozen law enforcement officers emerged from the blackness, following the beams of light to their target. Two of them quickly pounced on Sebrian, restraining him with handcuffs and frisking for additional weapons.

Only now did Harrison feel secure enough to fully appear from behind his shelter. And then he heard a very different sound coming from the night.

"Oh my God, Barre. Are you alright?"

The sound of Celeste's voice was both shocking and soothing. How did she get here? Is she OK? Where did all these police come from? Harrison's questions quickly faded at the moment he noticed the outline of her figure running toward him. He instinctively began heading for her, and the two embraced, long and deep.

"Thank God, Barre. I thought we'd be too late."

"Well, another few seconds and you might have been. But how did you know?"

"Surely you knew I'd find the sign you left at one of the caves, the one saying you were captive? The rest I just pieced together. If someone was holding you hostage, there could be only one reason. I just had to convince the police that this was really happening and that your life could be in danger."

"Howdy, folks." It was Ranger Rick, the local naturalist. "I'm sure glad everyone's OK."

Celeste continued her explanation. "I asked Rick if he would lead us out here since I knew it was likely you'd have to come at nighttime and I wasn't sure if I could find the way. He was incredibly helpful."

"I sure appreciate it," Harrison said, reaching out his arm to shake Ranger Rick's hand.

"No problem at all. My only question now is … did you find anything?"

With all the emotions Harrison had been coping with, he literally forgot about the buried chest, lying in a hole just yards from where they stood.

Harrison looked into Celeste's eyes. He saw the sympathy within, clearly directed at him and the lost quest for a buried treasure. "It's alright, Barre. Time to go home now."

Harrison responded in his usual dead-pan manner. "Yeah, I guess you're right. Too bad, though. I sure would've liked to see what is in that old chest buried over there. Maybe some other time," and he started to walk away.

Celeste yanked on his arm to stop his progress. Harrison turned back toward her. "What did you say?" Celeste muttered, her eyes wide and mouth slightly agape.

"I said it would have been nice to find out what's in the buried chest I found. But I guess we should get going now." He again turned to walk away.

This time Celeste grabbed his shirt and pulled him back toward her with unexpected strength. "Hold on there, Mr. Barrett. Start explaining."

Harrison figured he better explain before Celeste really got upset. "I was able to follow the rest of the clues that were on the original map taken from Alex Moreno's home. They lead to this spot right over here where I dug. Surprising how much you can accomplish with a gun pointed at your head."

Harrison led Celeste, Ranger Rick, and three of the police officers to the hole. Everyone now stood open-mouthed as they viewed the top of a wooden chest. Harrison hopped down into the hole. "Can you hand me the pickaxe, please," he motioned to Ranger Rick.

Rick passed him the pick and Harrison wedged the head underneath the front latch of the chest. With one forceful, yet precise, movement, he rocked the pick handle forward and watched the latch snap open.

The flashlights of the officers lit up the surface of the chest as if they were spotlights on a stage. And those standing on the rim of the hole were brimming with anxiety while awaiting the curtain to rise. Harrison bent onto one knee and grasped the latch with one hand and the side of the chest top with the other.

Harrison paused. No one moved. No one uttered a sound.

He looked back up at Celeste. As they exchanged glances, they also silently shared the memories of the past several weeks, from the death of a young boy to the near death of Harrison, himself.

Harrison turned back toward the chest, took a deep breath … and lifted the top.

EPILOGUE

THE SUN BEGAN TO PEEK through the curtains in Harrison's bedroom. Outside was the familiar sound of a lawn mower from one of his neighbors who liked to get his Saturday morning chores out of the way a little too early.

While lying in bed staring at the ceiling, Harrison's thoughts flashed back to the events of a few months ago. The tragic death of Alex Moreno that led to the adventure of a lifetime seemed so distant. Yet, its conclusion was still vivid in his mind and he could see every detail – as he lifted the lid of the buried chest, the flashlight beams illuminated the golden metal within, mirroring the sparkle of the stars directly above.

Everyone at the scene stood gawking, dumbfounded, until Harrison spoke, "So ... do you think this is the John Marsh treasure everyone's been looking for?"

The weeks following the remarkable discovery were a blur. The news media was relentless with interview requests. The story was even picked up nationally and Harrison and Celeste were transformed into local celebrities. The free coffee from the Brentwood Starbucks was an especially appreciated perk.

And, of course, there were the attorneys. The State Park Service took the lead in sorting out who would get what share. By the time the estimates were finalized, the value was staggering. Just as Celeste hypothesized, the John Marsh treasure was in the form of gold coins; one-thousand-eight-hundred-and seventy-five of the rare *$20 Liberty 'No Motto'* coins minted in San Francisco circa 1850. The auction houses placed the total value at around thirty-three million dollars.

The settlement, however, was surprisingly quick and free from bickering. The Marsh family heirs all agreed to donate most of their share back to the State Park Service for the restoration and maintenance of the Old Stone House. Along with the State Park's own percentage, there appeared to be plenty of money to return the Stone House to its former glory as well as create a living museum and interpretive center on the grounds.

The Great Stone House would once again stand tall and proud in the shadow of Diablo, beckoning visitors to explore its secrets.

However, the portion of the treasure that most satisfied Harrison was the agreed upon half-million dollars that went to the family of Alex Moreno for use as a college fund for his sister, Gabrielle. Tears still welled in his eyes as he lay in bed reflecting on the irony of Alex's death, thankful that he was able to help provide some closure for the family.

Harrison was also in a state of surreal disbelief at his share of the fortune. Though he declined to negotiate for any amount, he was issued a standard finder's fee of ten percent. Over three million dollars. The number still was unreal. He was a teacher, after all. Always was. Always would be. What in the world would he do with three million dollars?

THE RISING SUN CONTINUED TO FILL the room with a warm glow. In his contemplation, Harrison let a grin arch across his face. He realized that, in the end, he had discovered something much more valuable than gold.

A sense of contentment overwhelmed him and he shook the thoughts of the past from his mind. Rolling to his side, he gently stretched out his arm and placed it on top of the soft, warm shoulder lying next to him. "How are you feeling?" Harrison asked quietly.

Celeste grasped his hand and wrapped it around her. "Like a …" She paused and inhaled deeply, then with a soft sigh and slight smile replied, "… *Wakatanka.*"

Mt. Diablo[14]

END NOTES

The previous story is a combination of fact and fiction. The general details surrounding the lives of John and Charles Marsh are historically accurate. The John Marsh Stone House can be seen today, part of the California State Park system on the outskirts of the city of Brentwood. Vasco Caves, with its vernal pools and Indian pictographs, is accessible by guided tour. And of course, the peaks of Mt. Diablo are easily visible throughout the San Francisco Bay Area.

The legend of the John Marsh gold has existed for decades, since, perhaps, prior to Marsh's death. Should it be more than just a legend, it is not surprising that a treasure hidden somewhere on the once sprawling 40,000 acre Rancho Los Meganos has yet to be discovered. Those readers that believe a tale of buried gold coins is too farfetched are encouraged to research the Saddle Ridge Hoard, discovered less than a year after this novel's initial publication. A coincidence?

Below are the bibliographic citations for the images and letters used herein and reprinted with permission. For more information about the remarkable life of John Marsh, the reader is encouraged to visit the website for the John Marsh Historic Trust at www.johnmarshhouse.com.

1. Page16. John Marsh Stone House. 1856. John Marsh Collection. East Contra Costa Historical Society and Museum. Brentwood, CA. Photographic print.

2. Page 32. John Marsh and Miwoks. Oil on canvas painted c.1934. WPA Artwork. H. Ridyer. From the estate of Roy E. and Thelma D. Thorton. On loan from Michael and Joyce Tracy to the East Contra Costa Historical Society and Museum. Brentwood, CA.

3. Page 47. John Marsh Letter to Samuel Tuck. June 12, 1855. Marsh Family Papers. Bancroft Library. UC Berkeley.

4. Page 49. John Marsh Letter to Samuel Tuck. Aug. 18, 1855. Marsh Family Papers. Bancroft Library. UC Berkeley.

5. Page 50. John, Abby, and Alice Marsh. c. 1854. John Marsh Collection. East Contra Costa Historical Society and Museum. Brentwood, CA. Photographic print.

6. Page 65. Marsh Family Journal. John Marsh Collection. East Contra Costa Historical Society and Museum. Brentwood, CA.

7. Page 84. John Marsh. c. 1855. John Marsh Collection. East Contra Costa Historical Society and Museum. Brentwood, CA. Photographic print.

8. Page 104. John Marsh with Miwok and Vaqueros. Oil on canvas painted c. 1934. WPA Artwork. H. Ridyer. From the estate of Roy E. and Thelma D. Thorton. On loan

from Michael and Joyce Tracy to the East Contra Costa Historical Society and Museum. Brentwood, CA.

9. Page 121. Charles Marsh. c. 1860. John Marsh Collection. East Contra Costa Historical Society and Museum. Brentwood, CA. Photographic print.

10. Page 173. John Marsh Stone House. c. 1870. John Marsh Collection. East Contra Costa Historical Society and Museum. Brentwood, CA. Photographic print.

11. Page 184. The Head of Joaquin Murrieta Poster. 1853. Photo Collection. Los Angeles Public Library. Los Angeles, CA. Print reproduction.

12. Page 216. Native American Bird Pictograph from Vasco Caves. Date unknown. Sketch reproduction (upper circles not part of original cave drawing).

13. Page 237. Alice Cameron Marsh. c. 1870. Marsh Family Papers. Bancroft Library. UC Berkeley. Portrait on Ivory.

14. Page 267. Mt. Diablo. 2012. Photograph by Veronica Hanel